THE COMPLETE CASES
OF BOOKIE BARNES

THE COMPLETE CASES OF

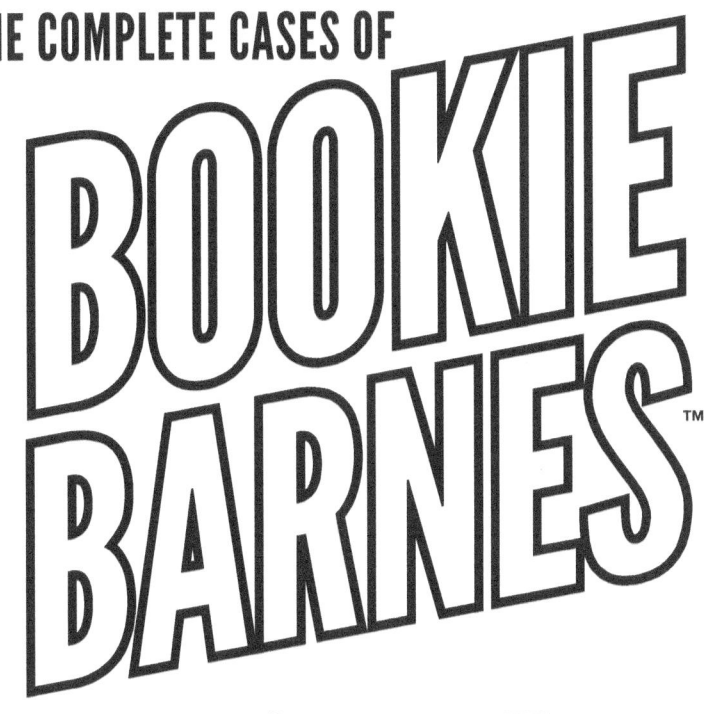

BOOKIE BARNES™

ROBERT REEVES

INTRODUCTION BY
GARY HOPPENSTAND

PRIMARY ILLUSTRATORS
PETE KUHLHOFF
RAFAEL DESOTO

POPULAR PUBLICATIONS • 2021

TABLE OF CONTENTS

INTRODUCTION BY
GARY HOPPENSTAND

PULP CRIME fiction author, Robert Reeves, introduces his truck-driving protagonist in the story "Murder in High Gear" (*Black Mask* magazine, August 1941) as follows: "The boys called him Bookie Barnes not because he made book but because they suspected that he once read one." Of the many crime fiction protagonists in pulp magazine fiction, perhaps none is more unique than Bookie Barnes. A truck driver employed by Murdock Motor Freight, Barnes is a tough working class hero. Though not a detective *per se*, he is a rough customer described as "tall, heavy-chested, with a build you see only in physical culture ads, and, though barely twenty-six, he'd been on the trucks for three years." He is emblematic of the type of crime fighters found in pulp fiction in that he represents the typical readership of pulp fiction: an average working-class audience.

When thinking of pulp detective fiction during the 1920s, 1930s, and 1940s, many of the detectives were working class. The most famous detectives of the golden age of pulp fiction (the 1920s and 1930s), including Dashiell Hammett's Sam Spade and Continental Op, and Raymond Chandler's Philip Marlowe, are working-class professional private investigators. There were some aristocrat pulp crime fighters of that period (The Shadow and The Spider spring immediately to mind), but most were characteristic of the readers who plunked down that dime for an issue of the pulp fiction magazine's brand of escapism.

Regarding the social class of the pulp fiction magazine reader and writer, Erin A. Smith states:

> Because writer's lives and readers' lives were in some way homologous, there was a good symbolic fit between the attitudes and values of the white working men who read the pulps and the pulp-fiction forms they appropriated to express and reinforce their worldviews (26).

Dime Detective Magazine was the perfect pulp fiction venue for these readers. James L. Traylor makes the spot-on point that "[*Dime Detective Magazine*] continued to sell because of its characters. Some were gimmicky and far fetched: however, they captured the fancy of the readership" (iii). Traylor also suggests that *Dime Detective Magazine* started as "a direct imitation of *Black Mask*" (*Dime Detective Companion,* 1), which was the premiere detective pulp fiction magazine of its time.

But what made Bookie Barnes unique among the stable of detectives published in *Dime Detective Magazine* was that he was the embodiment of the common working man caught in criminal situations. In a number of ways, he is, as Albert Camus stated, "A man who has become conscious of the absurd [and] is forever bound to it" (Duncan, 7). Barnes is simply a truck driver (though a tough-guy individual) who is doing his job. His encounters with crime has about them an absurdist element, and reinforces a rather grim depiction of the greed and avarice of the human condition. Through it all, he overcomes the absurd, solves the crime, and returns to his job. My guess is that American working-class readers strongly empathized with this type of hero, during an era coming out of the Great Depression and entering the cataclysmic global events of Word War II. He proves that no matter what station in life a blue-collar worker exists, that the rational can overcome the irrationality of crime and violence with toughness and clear-headedness. Sadly, Robert Reeves published only three Bookie Barnes tales in his very concise writing career

Not much is known about Robert Reeves' (1911/12–1945) short writing stint in the pulps. Some information (if it can be trusted) may be gleaned from the dustjacket back cover blurbs from two of this three novels. The back cover dustjacket of *No Love Lost* (1941), his second mystery novel featuring his protagonist Cellini Smith, states that he learned his writing skills "in the hard school." Reeves own statement claims that he was 29 years old at the time of publication of *No Love Lost,* and that he was "currently wedded only to [his] writing." He stated that his childhood was in the "East" and that we worked a variety of jobs. The blurb goes on to state that he received a degree from New York University, and that he had an interest in the theater, working as a stage manager, play doctor, and casting director, involved in nearly every aspect of the theatrical profession. The statement goes on to say "he heard the call of the West," and moved to Los Angeles, an experience that he uses as background information in *No Love Lost.* The blurb concludes with a statement that his ambition was to "travel to South America."

The back cover blurb of the dust jacket found on his third published hardcover novel, *Cellini Smith* (1943), provides additional information about Reeves. He stated that he enlisted in the U.S. Army on July 22, 1942, as what his mother called a "Private Buck." Regarding this period, he said:

I doubt if it's necessary (or even permissible) to explain the processing that goes on in [military] induction centers. I punch typewriters, pick up forms, put them down, etc. My commanding officer tells me to write a book about the place (as I intend to), but wisely adds that I wait till the war is won.

Sadly, Reeves never had the opportunity to write that book. Repeating his description of his life in New York City, he adds that he left the theater to become a writer, and that he was working on a fourth novel. He described himself as being thirty years old at the time of the publication of *Cellini Smith,* and depreciatingly describes his physical appearance as "growing bald at an alarming rate." The blurb concludes with his vision of what he wanted to do with his life after World War II was over, a life that tragically was cut short during the war, claiming that his ambition was to "march down *Unter Den Linden* and then get me a thirty-foot twin-screw boat strictly for fishing purposes." Such was not to be. The world of crime fiction would never see the potential work of this truly talented writer. Of course, one should always be suspect of an author's biography as a back-cover blurb, but these revelations about the writer do reveal a certain element of humor in his view of life.

In an article published in the Spring 1985 issue of *The Armchair Detective,* critic John L. Apostolou states: "Of the eleven short stories Robert Reeves wrote for the pulps, seven feature Cellini Smith. All seven are set in Los Angeles, and most of them are mildly comic" (187). He goes on to say that: "The fiction of Robert Reeves is worthy of further discussion" (187). Never were truer words spoken. Reeves' untimely death is somewhat unclear during World War II in the 500th Bomber Squadron of the U.S. Military fighting in the South Pacific. As Apostolou notes:

"...official records show that he died on July 11, 1945, only a month before the war ended... Reeves held the rank of captain... [his remains] re-interred in 1950, at Fort McPherson National Cemetery, near North Platte, Nebraska..." (188).

Bookie Barnes, as the existential work-class hero, making sense out of the social cancer of crime, left us with way too few tales of his adventures, just as his creator, Robert Reeves, did for his crime fiction in general. Enjoy these three Bookie Barnes stories, including the non-series story, "Dance Macabre," which introduces a somewhat darker view of crime than did his Cellini Smith adventures.

WORKS CITED

Apostolou, John L. "The Short Career of Robert Reeves." *The Armchair Detective*, Spring 1985, ed. Michael Seidman. (New York: *The Armchair Detective*, pp. 185–188).

Duncan, Paul. *Noir Fiction: Dark Highways*. (Harpenden, Herts, U.K.: 2000).

Traylor, James L. *Dime Detective Companion*. (Boston: Altus Press, 2011).

—— *Dime Detective Index*. (New Carrollton, Maryland: The Pulp Collector Press, 1986).

Smith, Erin A. *Hard-Boiled: Working-Class Readers and Pulp Magazines*. (Philadelphia: Temple University Press, 2000).

MURDER IN HIGH GEAR

INTRODUCING BOOKIE BARNES, DAUNTLESS KNIGHT OF THE HIGHWAY. DETECTIVES AND DAMES, SNOWBIRDS AND SNOWSTORMS, THEY'RE ALL THE SAME TO BOOKIE WHEN HE MOUNTS HIS TWELVE-TON CHARGER AND BEARS DOWN ON A MODERN DRAGON IN THE FORM OF A NARCOTIC-SMUGGLING SET-UP, IN WHICH THE HEROINE TURNS OUT TO BE A DOPE—AND THE DOPE TURNS OUT TO BE HEROIN.

CHAPTER ONE
SOUTHBOUND

HE TURNED his back on the twenty-mile wind, cupped his hands and when he succeeded in lighting a cigarette on the third try he resumed his rapid stride for the wide, brick building at the end of the block. He drew deeply on the cigarette, holding it so that its glowing end nearly touched the skin of his palm. It was bitterly cold and the wind cut through his leather windbreaker as if it were a beauty contest winner's costume.

It had stopped snowing and he didn't like it. It was better to drive the trucks in any slush or snow or sleet than in this sort of weather. This kind of freezing wind was turning the snow into ice and the tractor and trailer would slide like soap in a wet fist. He wished he was pulling into the New York terminal already.

He was tall, heavy-chested, with a build you see only in physical culture ads, and, though barely twenty-six, he'd been on the trucks for three years. He was a good driver and pinned to his peaked cap was a silver button—the insignia of two years' continuous driving without a single accident.

The boys called him Bookie Barnes not because he made book but because they suspected that he once read one. However, he didn't mind the monicker—he'd long since given up trying to convince the boys that he was pitched

At the same instant, Bookie whirled on the gorilla next to him and his foot kicked out—

out of college in his third year for flunking a dead language in a lively fashion.

He reached the brick building that housed the Bridgeport terminal of Murdock Motor Freight, Inc., and entered the office. He pulled his time card from the rack, punched it and slipped it into a deep pocket of his jacket. It was 10:58 p.m.

He turned to leave the office when he was suddenly arrested by a slight noise. He snapped on the ceiling lights and looked past the wooden balustrade that separated the passageway from the main part of the office.

A stranger, bent over a waste-paper basket, straightened up and returned Bookie Barnes' stare. He was thin and lanky and fleshless—certainly not a truck driver. In his

hands were a couple of discarded trip meter cards and he now dropped these back into the basket.

"If it's the safe you're looking for," said Bookie, "it's over in the corner there."

"Thank you," replied the stranger. "I'll get my drill."

Bookie Barnes pushed open the door that led into the terminal and yelled: "Hey, Bill!" He didn't take his eyes off the stranger.

A moment later, Bill Connelly, foreman for Murdock Motor Freight, answered the call. He was a beefy specimen with that lumbering flatfooted quality that most truckmen acquire after years in the game.

Bookie said: "I caught this toothpick snooping in here."

The stranger calmly lit a cigarette, his eyes staring at the foreman's bare arms with their rolled-up sleeves.

"Forget it," said Bill Connelly to Bookie Barnes. "I know about him."

"Those scratches on your arm. How'd you get them?" The stranger's voice was cold, slightly bored.

"I was playing with my kitten before I came down here tonight," replied the foreman. "Why?"

"Nothing. Just wondering."

Bill Connelly turned on his heels and walked out.

BOOKIE BARNES followed the foreman through the door into the immense place that served as garage, warehouse, and repair shop. The place was the usual nightly madhouse before the departure of the semi-trailers—those pachyderms of the highway consisting of a huge trailer and a powerful tractor to pull it.

Sweating, swearing men on the platform loaded consignments into the enormous, yellow-painted jobs. Drivers wrestled with skid chains as they worked them onto the large, double tires. Cranes that swung from the steel beams in the ceiling were shifting heavy crates along the platform, motors were being tuned and tractors were being eased around in incredibly small areas and coupled to their trailers.

Bookie Barnes agreed with some of the boys that it was as cold as a traffic cop's heart and waved to Jeff and Dutchy who were shooting craps for a pair of fleece-lined gloves. Then he jumped on the platform and sought out the foreman.

"Did I pull a boner with that skeleton in the office?" asked Bookie.

"It makes no difference," shrugged Bill Connelly. "I wish I knew what he wanted, anyway."

"Don't you know?"

"No." Bill Connelly sounded worried. "Mr. Murdock just told me to give him what he wants and I'm not gonna argue with the boss. He asked for a ride into New York."

"I hope I don't draw him," said Bookie Barnes.

"I'm sending him with Latch."

"Fine. What job do I take?"

Bill Connelly jerked a finger at one of the aluminium bodies the men were still loading. "That there. And don't try to be any Sonja Henie with her. Just take it easy."

"Having trouble tonight?"

"Trouble!" The foreman's tomato-red face grew even redder. "I got two breakdowns waiting for me right now and Slim just called from outside Westport. He tried to do a rumba with a telegraph pole. I'm gonna be on the road all night just because you bums want to save gas and skid into New York."

Bookie Barnes promised to be careful and asked: "What tractor do I take—number eleven?"

"No. Yours'll be six. I haven't got a trip meter card in eleven yet."

Bookie looked it over. "Damn it, Bill, that job hasn't even got chains on her."

"Well, what do you want on her?" roared the irritated foreman. "Slave bracelets? Get going."

Bookie Barnes swore under his breath and jumped off the platform. Chaining those wheels was always a messy business. For a half-hour he worked and sweated. The semi-trailers rumbled out for all points of the compass. Bill Connelly got another call that Mike Projak was trying to spin his wheels out of an ice-hardened ditch. He donned his mackinaw and left in a sedan loaded down with gunny sacks for traction, spare lanterns, and repair kits. Jeff finally won the gloves from Dutchy and they went on their trucks.

Latch, a wildcat truck operator from the old days, began moving out with eleven and stuck his head out of the cab as he passed Bookie Barnes. "See you at the Derby."

Bookie nodded. Latch moved on, tooted his horn as he passed the office door, and the stranger came out and swung into the cab and they left. Bookie Barnes finished his job, got into the cab and neatly maneuvered the tractor in front of the trailer. He got off, locked down the supports which coupled trailer to tractor and connected the hoses on either side which automatically released the vacuum trailer brakes.

The trailer was loaded by now. He checked the twenty-seven red, green, and yellow lights and the six reflectors, found them in order, hauled himself into the cab and the semi-trailer started moving out of Murdock Motor Freight's Bridgeport terminal, southbound for New York.

BOOKIE BARNES turned right from State onto the Boston Post Road. The cab, at least, was warm from the engine but the road was worse than he had expected. The driving wind had wash-boarded the snow in many spots, making the trailer swing like a cooch dancer's hips. He kept the tractor in third, not daring to hit high.

He crawled along, leaving Bridgeport and entering the outskirts of Fairfield when he sighted a string of red lanterns that signified a stranded truck. It was one of Murdock's screaming-yellow jobs and he slowed down.

Bill Connelly and Mike Projak were still trying to get the semi-trailer out of a shallow ditch. The foreman waved Bookie Barnes to a halt as he came up.

"That damn friend of the boss's don't want to ride with Latch. You pick him up at the Stink House and drive him in."

Bookie Barnes said he would, shifted into first with his feet and trundled off. He didn't mind having a passenger. Ordinarily, they were a nuisance but this particular one had aroused his curiosity. Friends of the boss didn't customarily search trash baskets.

A couple of minutes later he reached the lunch wagon the drivers called the Stink House, stopped in back of a Mack and hopped off the cab. A small figure emerged from behind the Mack and blocked his path. The figure wore a next year's model in camel's hair coat and the dim light from the lunch wagon's windows showed a round, oily-complexioned face.

"Sorry," said Bookie Barnes. "No riders." He made to go but the figure didn't budge. "Listen, greaseball, you heard me the first time."

"Sure," said the greaseball. "Sure I heard you—Bookie.

"How the hell do you know my name?"

"I just made a lucky guess, Bookie," the other said confidently.

"Make another guess what I'll do if you don't get out of my way."

The greaseball looked up at the towering figure and nodded. "You got a good chest and good arms, Bookie, and you could split me like a wishbone. I'd be duck soup for you. But you wouldn't put a meathook on me. You educated guys like to think you got a sense of honor and you never sock anybody that's smaller. That's where we got the jump on you."

Bookie frowned, his hands itching. He had the feeling that the greaseball was trying to stall for time. He said: "Don't be so sure."

"I'm positive," the greaseball replied. He didn't sound afraid. "You said you don't take riders, Bookie. Then how come you're goin' inside there to pick one up? If you—"

He broke off as a dual-axle tanker, with a couple of drivers inside, rolled up. He muttered something under his breath, wheeled and disappeared in the darkness.

Bookie stared after him reflectively, then entered the Stink House.

YOU COULD cut the air with a lady-finger, and the broom ostentatiously resting in a far corner was purely ornamental. It was one of those numerous lunch wagons along the road that cater to truck trade and nothing else.

Bookie Barnes spotted the stranger and walked over. "Bill Connelly asked me to stop by and haul you into town," he said.

"Fine," replied the stranger. He didn't seem to recognize Bookie from their previous meeting.

Jeff and Dutchy, who were straddling nearby counter stools, became interested. "You a friend of Bill's?" asked Jeff.

"No." The stranger's voice was curt and sharp and his eyes sized up the driver with suspicion.

Dutchy dug his companion in the ribs. "My, but we're touchy tonight, ain't we?"

"Then how come you rate a lift?" pursued Jeff. "We ain't allowed to carry no riders."

"The owner of your firm, Mr. Murdock, said I could get a lift. Satisfied now?"

"Sure," said Jeff slowly. "But you're too skinny to be so touchy. Ain't he too skinny, Dutchy?"

"Sure," agreed the other. "You could lift him up by the navel with one finger."

"The little finger?" asked Jeff with mock awe.

"I don't know about that," Dutchy considered. "My pinky has always been kind of weak."

The stranger smiled contemptuously, his hands thrust deep in his overcoat pockets. He nodded to Jeff. "Why are your eyes so narrowed. Do you have to wear glasses or is there something else that's wrong?"

Jeff blinked with surprise, then moved forward. Bookie Barnes lunged between them, planted a huge palm in Jeff's face and pushed back. The rest of the drivers brightened at the prospect of a free-for-all.

Bookie said quickly: "Let's get going."

The stranger shrugged and walked out with unhurried steps. Bookie Barnes followed him, they got into the cab and started off.

"Jeff didn't mean any harm," said Bookie.

"It's all right."

Their voices were pitched high to dominate the artillery sound of the motor. "My name is Barnes," said Bookie and paused expectantly for the other's reply.

The stranger didn't bother to supply his own name. "Do you make this trip to New York regularly?"

"Yes, I'm on it steady. You know, it's peculiar about you." Bookie's eyes were on the road.

"What is?" Again the stranger's voice had that tinge of suspicion.

"That Connelly asked me especially to stop by the Stink House and haul you into town."

"What about it?"

"Most of the other boys there are going on to New York," said Bookie, "and they could have hauled you in just as well."

"I asked Connelly to go with you."

"How come? You don't even know me."

"That's right," stated the stranger carefully. "I don't even know you."

Bookie Barnes frowned as he pulled up at the Derby but then shrugged. It was none of his business. "How about a coffee?" he asked.

"How come you didn't have it at the other place?" countered the stranger.

"I always make my two stops here and at a place in Greenwich when I go to New York. Drivers never like to change their stops." He started to get out, then added: "Another thing. Boss's friend or not—you're too damned close-mouthed yourself to get nosey about me. Remember that."

The stranger smiled, put a cigarette into his mouth and began to hunt for matches.

BOOKIE BARNES entered the Derby, which was neither more nor less dirty than the other, and sat down next to Latch who was chewing at a Broadway Crunch Bar. One other man sat at the opposite end of the counter. A queer feeling came over Bookie when he sighted the man. It was the greaseball.

Bookie ordered coffee and refused a piece of Latch's candy.

"I guess there are better nickel bars," said the truck-shaped truck driver judiciously. "These can't hold a candle to the Clipper Almond Cluster."

"Uh-huh," agreed Bookie absently.

"Of course the Cluster don't last long enough between stops. If you regard it that way, the Honeycomb Nonpareil gives you the best buy for your jitney."

"Sure." Bookie swallowed the mud-colored hot water, dropped a nickel on the counter and stood up.

"Shoving off so quickly?" asked the surprised Latch.

"Yes. The roads are lousy and I don't want to have to make time."

"O.K. See you at Delmonico's."

"Besides," said Bookie Barnes, "I got that boss's friend for a rider. We haven't started yet and we aren't on speaking terms already."

"Say," asked Latch, "did you draw that string bean?"

"Yes. How come he didn't stay with you?"

"That guy's plain nuts, Bookie. I stopped to see if I could help Mike Projak out of that ditch and this string bean got out with me and then when we were getting back into the cab he just ups and tells Connelly he don't want to go with me." Latch bit viciously into the Broadway Crunch Bar.

"Something's damned funny," said Bookie Barnes and started for the door when the greaseball's voice stopped him.

"What's the rush, Bookie? You got a lot of brains. You oughta know rushing ain't good for the digestion."

Bookie Barnes sighed. "Latch," he asked with disgust, "what can I do about a termite like that?"

The greaseball stood up and walked over, his teeth framed in all their yellow glory in a wide grin.

Latch said: "You might start by cooling him off with that water."

Bookie reached for a glass of water on the counter and his wrist snapped. The greaseball did not flinch or move a step as the water slapped his face and body. The grin even seemed to widen. "Sure, you'd try some thing like that," remarked the swarthy little man. "But like I told you, you're too lousy with honor to sock me."

"I ain't," Latch put in. "I'd be glad to sock you."

The greaseball regarded Latch and his hands went into the pockets of his camel's hair coat. "I guess you would. You ain't got brains like King Kong here so you got to use your fists. But you still ain't gonna make a pass at me because you're scared I might have my mitt on a heater inside my pocket."

Latch didn't move. The hash-slinger behind the counter made some remark about no gunplay and the greaseball sat down on his stool and wiped his face with a paper napkin.

Bookie Barnes studied the oily-faced man. Something eluded him—something that might explain the grease-ball's actions. Finally he shrugged, nodded to Latch and opened the door.

In an unnecessarily loud voice, the greaseball yelled: "What's the hurry?"

"Don't stretch your luck too far," said Bookie. He went outside, climbed into the cab, turned over the motor and the semi-trailer started off again.

The stranger leaned against the far corner of the cab and stared ahead down the Post Road without making any comment. They moved along slowly, for some time, the twelve rolling tons feeling treacherously light under Bookie's hands. He hugged the right, his eyes glued to the road, cursing as cars went by without cutting their brights.

Bookie Barnes would have liked to talk and he was sorry that he and the stranger had not hit it off better. The slow going began to irk him and he carefully slipped into high. He rounded a curve and as he straightened out he hit a stretch of washboarded ice and, with a crazy, drunken motion, the trailer suddenly careened to the right, sending the tractor sliding leftward. The movement was slow and graceful—and deadly.

Bookie Barnes arrested his instinctive lunge for the brakes, instead stepped up the speed a couple of notches. The giant vehicle swayed over to the other side, shuddered gently and straightened out again. He allowed the semi-trailer to slow down, slammed it back into second gear, then took a deep breath. Tiny, icy fingers seemed to drum up and down his spine as he thought of what would have happened had any cars been coming in the opposite direction. Luck had been with him.

For the first time, Bookie Barnes noticed that the lurching vehicle had thrown the stranger up against him. He nudged the man with his arm.

"Sorry, but you're crowding me."

The stranger didn't budge. Bookie Barnes pulled over to the side and stopped. He picked up a heavy flashlight on the seat beside him and played it over the stranger's face.

He was as dead as international law.

CHAPTER TWO
OUT OF THE NIGHT

THE SIREN, decided Bookie Barnes, was definitely a silly business when you were crawling after a motor-cycle cop at the rate of twelve miles an hour. He was following Joe, an old friend of his on the Southport force. They were coming into Southport now and in a couple of minutes the cop skidded to a halt in front of a small all-night clinic.

Bookie Barnes stopped, opened the cab door and hauled out the stranger. He weighed more than he looked and there was a feel of solid muscle about the skinny body. He followed Joe, carrying his burden up the steps. Bookie Barnes didn't mind death—he'd seen too much of it at its messiest. The only thing that could still get him was seeing a kid flattened out.

Only a young interne was on duty in the clinic. Trying his best to appear nonchalant, he produced a spanking new stethoscope and bent over the body that Bookie deposited on the porcelain table.

The interne listened a while, then said: "He's dead."

Joe nodded. "That's very clever of you, son. Now how about telling us why the guy cashed in."

"It would require an autopsy to ascertain that," replied the interne frigidly.

"You seen too many Kildare pictures, son." The cop took out pad and pencil. "What happened, Bookie?"

"I had him as a rider and a couple of miles back, coming around that curve by the Shell station, I went into a skid. It nearly scared the pants off me but it looks like it scared everything off this guy."

"It could have been heart failure," put in the interne.

For the next twenty minutes the cop plied Bookie Barnes with more questions, made notes and prepared a preliminary statement. A call was put through to Murdock Motor Freight in search of Bill Connelly but the foreman was still out on the road.

Finally, Joe pulled reflectively at the lobe of an ear and said: "Guess there's no use holding you up any longer, Bookie. It sure looks like heart failure and we got a lot of things to do. When you pull into your New York office give us a ring and we'll tell you what time we want you down here."

"I wish to hell I was in New York already," said Bookie Barnes fervently.

He went outside and got into the cab. He began to run over the starter when he noticed a sheet of paper on the seat beside him. It must have slipped out of the stranger's pocket when he'd carried him into the clinic. Bookie lit a match and examined the writing on the paper. It proved to be a complete list of the Murdock Motor Freight drivers and his own name headed the list.

WESTPORT WAS not a customary coffee-and-an-chor stop for Bookie but tonight he had news. It was a half-hour after he left the Southport clinic that he pulled up behind some other truck units at a place in Westport the boys called the Waldorf. It was an unsavory duplicate of the other lunch wagons.

News travels fast on the Road and in a code all its own. A wig-wagging light, a swerving wheel or fingers and hands held in certain ways out of windows are all part of the truck driver's language. In this case, Steve Czerno had spotted the semi-trailer in front of the clinic and had flagged the information to Dutchy and Jeff and others—and all were waiting, knowing full well that Bookie would put in an appearance at the Waldorf.

Preoccupied with his thoughts, Bookie Barnes entered, sat down at the counter and ordered coffee. Something nagged at him—those questions the dead stranger had asked about eyes and about the scratches the kitten had made on the foreman's arm.

"Look at the lousy prima donna," complained Dutchy. "He wants roses laid at his feet because he socked some bindlestiff and took him to the clinic."

"I didn't sock anybody," said Bookie.

"Then what were you doing there?"

"I made a figure eight back by that Shell curve," explained Bookie Barnes, "and that skeleton I had riding with me cashed in." He snapped his fingers. "Just like that—without waiting for any change."

The drivers regarded Bookie with respect. "Hell," one of them finally said, "that ain't a laughing matter. Did his neck break or something?"

"No. His ticker just gave out," Bookie said.

"A bag of bones like that guy shoulda been in a hospital to begin with," said a hatchet-pussed driver.

Bookie Barnes shook his head. "That string bean was just built skinny but he was heavier than he looked."

"That baby was much tougher than he looked," agreed Steve Czerno.

The others looked at him. "How come you know about him?" asked Bookie.

Steve Czerno looked sheepish. "I had a fight with him a couple of weeks ago but I never said nothing because he kind of made a monkey out of me."

"Are you sure it was the same guy?" Bookie asked.

"Pretty sure," replied Czerno. "I stopped at a place in Larchmont and when I come out I found this pair of stilts messing around in the back of my truck. I took a poke at him and the next thing I knew I was flat on my can and he dusted."

"What'd he want with your truck?" asked Dutchy.

"I was too busy trying to get up to ask him."

As the drivers digested this new item of information, the door pushed open and a uniformed cop entered. Those of the boys who knew him delivered a chorus of razzes.

The cop asked: "Which one of you kiddy car experts runs that number six Murdock outfit?"

"That's mine," said Bookie. "What about it?"

"Plenty," replied the cop. "Is your name Barnes?"

Bookie nodded.

"O.K. Come on down to the station. We got some questions to ask you."

"I'm busy," said Bookie. "I have to run a load into town. What is it about—that guy who died on my wagon?"

"Died my bustle," responded the cop. "He was murdered."

Bookie wasn't surprised. It was unreal, yet somehow inevitable.

BOOKIE BARNES and the cop entered the Westport police station and went over to the desk where sat Sergeant Button.

Bookie knew the sergeant—a tough veteran of the bootlegging era on the Post Road. At the moment, he was talking to Bill Connelly, foreman for Murdock Motor Freight.

"All right," the sergeant was saying, "we know you didn't kill the slob so stop thinking a half-hour before you answer a question. Now just why did you let this guy ride on your trucks?"

"It was none of my business," replied Connelly. "He showed up at the plant tonight with a letter from Mr. Murdock saying to take him to New York because he was a prospective customer and he wanted to check on the kind of service we had. It sounded phoney but it was no skin off my teeth. Besides," the foreman added, "he didn't look like no customer to me."

"What did he look like?"

"Just like a guy who wanted to bum a free ride."

"Um," said Sergeant Button. "And where's your boss now?"

"Mr. Murdock went to New York late this afternoon. He said he was flying to Washington on business."

"Do you know what airline he uses?"

The foreman supplied a name and the sergeant dispatched a cop to make a phone call, then turned to Bookie Barnes. "And what do you know about David Lindsay?"

"Is Lindsay his name?"

"Yes," nodded the sergeant. "The Fairfield police found a wallet on him with his name and stuff. When they found it was murder they asked us to pick you up for a few preliminary questions."

"How come he was murdered?" asked Bookie. "There wasn't even any blood."

"There wouldn't be," replied Sergeant Button. "Somebody buried an ice pick in Lindsay's back, right into his heart. The handle of the pick broke off so you couldn't see it and any little blood that came through was absorbed by his overcoat."

Bookie Barnes leaned back in his chair and absently lit a cigarette. It could have happened that way of course. With the blade of the pick remaining in Lindsay's back there wouldn't have been much blood. He tried to guess when it could have happened and wondered if Steve Czerno's fight with the murdered man a couple of weeks before had anything to do with it. He remembered the sheet of paper in his pocket and handed it to the sergeant.

Sergeant Button studied it and asked: "What's this?"

"It's a list of our drivers. I think it slipped out of Lindsay's pockets."

"Why is your name at the top?"

"Because the drivers' names are arranged alphabetically," responded Bookie.

"What do you think Lindsay wanted with a list like this?"

Bookie told him he couldn't guess. The cop who had left to make a phone call returned with the information that Mr. Murdock was due to land at the Washington airport within the hour and that they would contact him then.

Bookie Barnes said: "While you're at it there's a crumb you ought to try and pick up and question on the killing."

The sergeant picked up a pencil. "Let's have it."

"Belted camel's hair coat with no buttons and with raglan sleeves," said Bookie. "Tan shoes and a light gray fedora with rolled brim. About five feet three and a half and a hundred and thirty-six pounds and a pan like a can of putty with vaseline over it."

"That sounds strictly like Lennox Avenue," commented the sergeant. "O.K., Barnes, talk."

FOR FIFTEEN minutes Bookie gave his story. When he was finished, the sergeant scratched his chin thoughtfully and said: "So you claim that between the time you came out of the beanery in Fairfield and you found Lindsay dead you never spoke one word with him. Right?"

"That's right."

"You mean that's wrong because Lindsay was in no talking condition. He was killed while you were inside the lunch wagon."

"It could have happened that way—but why?"

"Listen, Bookie, you told me yourself that Lindsay got in your hair. Now isn't it possible you had a fight with the guy and sort of had an ice pack handy?"

Bookie Barnes shook his head.

Bill Connelly spat disgustedly. "You're wasting your time, Sarge. Bookie never even met Lindsay before and had no reason to kill him and if he did he wouldn't do it while the guy was on his own truck. Besides, Bookie's not the kind to stab someone in the back. He'd just slap him around with his meathooks."

"Nuts," said Sergeant Button. "I'm just trying to figure all the angles. Besides, it's my hunch this is a robbery case."

"You said yourself that Lindsay had his wallet on him," put in Bookie Barnes.

Sergeant Button nodded. "The murderer got scared and ran away without taking it. I figure it this way: you were inside and some panhandler came along and saw Lindsay in the truck and hit him for a handout. Lindsay told him to chase his tail and the panhandler got mad and stuck the ice pick in him and ran."

"Maybe," Bookie said doubtfully. He didn't add that if Lindsay had been quarreling with a panhandler he wouldn't have turned his back to get stabbed—or that the explanation omitted several significant peculiarities about Lindsay.

Latch walked in, masticating an Imperial Almond Nougat. "I seen Bookie's bus outside when I passed," he explained, "and figured something might be wrong."

"This is the driver Lindsay first asked to go with," Connelly told the police sergeant.

The sergeant said to Latch: "That rider you were supposed to take into town was murdered."

Latch blinked and a piece of Imperial Almond Nougat stuck in his throat. He coughed but didn't speak.

"How come you didn't know he was killed?" Sergeant Button asked shrewdly. "With all the stops you guys make, you know pretty near everything that happens."

Latch snorted. "In your hat, Button. I was trying to put in some miles and I didn't make any stops."

"O.K. We understand that Lindsay, the man who was killed, refused to go with you. Why?"

"I don't know," replied Latch. "I spotted Bill here trying to help Mike Projak on the road and stopped. And this Lindsay just ups and tells Bill he wants to go with another driver."

The foreman said: "That's just like I told you. Lindsay asked to ride with Bookie so I sent him to wait at a lunch wagon and that's where Bookie picked him up a little later."

Sergeant Button sighed. "This whole business sure smells from marinated herring."

"How about letting the boys get on?" asked the foreman. "You don't need them any more and I got a breakdown waiting at Stamford."

"Wait a second." The sergeant pulled over the phone and talked to the Fairfield police for several minutes before hanging up. "It's O.K. to go but they want Bookie there tomorrow morning at eleven thirty."

Bookie Barnes stood up.

"Just one more thing," said the sergeant. "How about hi-jackers? Maybe a gang wanted to hijack the stuff in Bookie's trailer outside Fairfield and Lindsay tried to stop them and was knocked off."

"Not a chance," replied the foreman. "The stuff in Book-ie's trailer is too clumsy and it ain't worth hijacking. Just some heavy piping, castings, and a few rolls of BX cable. That's all there's in it."

BOOKIE BARNES left the outskirts of Westport and rumbled on, entering a relatively desolate stretch of U.S. Highway 1. The road was lit by a three-quarter moon, the weather was still bitter cold and ice still sheeted the macadam. He drove cautiously, observing the passing scen-ery as if he expected, he knew not from where, some threat of danger.

Something abruptly clicked in his mind and he swore. He'd been a fool not to think of it before. It was clear now why David Lindsay had asked about those scratches on Bill's arm, about Jeff's narrowed eyes. The pupils in the eyes of an habitual drug taker contract and those scratches on the foreman's arm could easily be taken for pinpricks—the hypo marks on the arm of a drug addict.

Lindsay was looking for an addict among Murdock's drivers. That was why he had a list of their names. Perhaps he worked for the motor vehicle bureau or even the I.C.C.—the Interstate Commerce Commission. Proba-bly a dick.

Suddenly, the figure of a man appeared standing in the middle of the road some thirty feet ahead. He didn't move as the truck bore down on him and Bookie Barnes slammed on his brakes.

The man came over to the driver's side of the cab and stood up on the running board. "I'm in trouble," he said.

"What's the matter?" asked Bookie cautiously.

"Something's wrong with my motor. I don't know what. How about trying to help me fix it?"

Bookie could see the outlines of a station wagon parked at the side with no lights. He shook his head. "Nothing doing. I'm not a mechanic and besides I'm late now."

The man beckoned with his hand in the window opening.

"Come on, buddy. It's good for a five spot," he said.

Out of the corner of his eye, Bookie could see a few shadowy figures slumped deep in the seats inside the station wagon. His hand found the heavy searchlight beside him. "Nothing doing," he repeated.

"Pull over and get out." The man's voice was brittle, no longer coaxing. His hat brim was turned low and his eyebrows came together in a small clump over his nose.

Bookie Barnes saw the man's right arm move upward. He waited no longer. He brought his arm around and the searchlight's head crashed into the clump of hair over the bridge of the nose. Bushy-brows disappeared from the window.

From somewhere there was a shout and the sound of running feet but Bookie was already in high, rolling along with no thought of the ice-sheeted road ahead.

He kept his eyes glued to the rear view mirror jutting out from the door hinge. He knew they were sure to follow. An open Fruehauf trailer-truck filled with slag rumbled by but other cars on the road were few. In the distance he could see the lights of the sleeping city of Norwalk.

Then, as he had expected, he began to see the dark, unlit shape of the station wagon closing in rapidly.

But suddenly, there sounded the strident scream of a police siren behind him and the pursuing station wagon disappeared from the mirror—probably down some side road.

CHAPTER THREE
HIGH GEAR

THE SOUND of the siren came in louder and a motorcycle cop drew abreast of the semi-trailer. The cop waved to Bookie to follow him and Bookie Barnes flickered his lights to say he understood. They reached the outskirts of Norwalk, rolled into the main drag and pulled up in front of the police station.

Bookie got out and joined the waiting cop. "Did you spot a station wagon back on the road there?" he asked.

The cop shook his head and they entered the station to find Steve Czerno being grilled by a big, competent-looking officer Bookie had never before seen. The man looked up and said: "Barnes? Glad you got here. I'm Lieutenant Hallery. Fairfield asked us to follow up a couple of things. Sit down."

Steve Czerno asked: "Do you need me any more?"

"No," replied the lieutenant, "but keep in touch with your office. We may want you later."

The truck driver nodded and lumbered out.

"What do you make of that guy?" asked Hallery.

"Steve?" said Bookie Barnes. "He's all right. A pretty good driver. Why?"

"We found out he had a fight with David Lindsay a couple of weeks ago and we had him picked up. Did you see him hanging around Fairfield when you were there?"

Bookie shook his head. "I didn't. He must have passed through before."

"All right." Hallery nodded to a nearby cop who went into an inner room. "Barnes," he continued, "we picked you up to make an identification."

The cop returned from the inner room, followed by the greaseball. The gray felt still sat jauntily on his head and the camel's hair coat was still belted around him in elegant, wasp-waist fashion.

"Is this the man?" asked the lieutenant.

Bookie Barnes nodded.

"Fine. What do you charge him with?"

"Charge him?" Bookie was surprised. "I've got a hunch he might be mixed up with the murder of David Lindsay."

"That's a fine thing," said Hallery angrily. "Turning the department upside down on account of a truck driver's hunch. While Lindsay was being murdered this man was inside the lunch wagon at Fairfield. We have the counter man's word for it and, in case you don't remember, you were there too."

"Then what did he want from me?" asked Bookie.

"It's no crime to try to get a ride from a truck driver," snapped the lieutenant. "His story is that his car stalled and he wanted a lift into New York but that he couldn't get it so he had his car fixed and went on—when we picked him up on your say-so."

Bookie said: "Then ask him if he knows anybody with bushy eyebrows who owns a station wagon."

"More of your damned hunches!" roared the lieutenant. "Stop talking in riddles. If you have any information or if you know who could have killed David Lindsay, say so!"

Bookie's weather-tanned face flushed red. He didn't like being pushed around. He said: "In that case I don't charge him with anything."

The lieutenant waved the greaseball away. "You can go now."

The small man looked at Bookie, his lips formed a soundless word of hate and he left.

HALLERY WAITED till the door closed behind the greaseball, then said: "Hereafter, Barnes, just keep your nose clean. Don't make baseless accusations and don't try to play detective either."

"Don't worry," said Bookie emphatically. "I'll make no more accusations."

"Good, because this case is a little bigger than you probably realize. David Lindsay worked for the government—narcotics."

Bookie Barnes whistled. This then was no small affair involving a truck driver who might be a drug addict.

The lieutenant stabbed a finger at a nearby cop. "Jones, get the trip record from the truck outside. If you have to break the lock it's all right."

Bookie asked. "How did you find out that Lindsay worked for the narcotics bureau?"

"Fairfield contacted your boss, Murdock, in Washington. He gave the information that Lindsay was a federal man."

"Did he say how we were mixed up in it?"

"He didn't know how much except that Lindsay came to him this afternoon about some kind of drug running. But you're on the wrong side, Barnes. It's me who should be doing the asking. Is there anything that you've conveniently forgotten?"

Bookie shook his head. "I told you all I knew when I asked you to pick up that greaseball."

The cop returned with a cardboard disc and placed it in front of Hallery. This was the semi-trailer's trip meter card. Most trucks are equipped with such a time recording device which consists essentially of a clock and a graph that records the driving time in tenths of an hour, the stops, and even gives a close indication of the rates of speed. It is a sealed, robot recorded that traces a driver's every move.

The lieutenant studied the card and the black, circular graph on it that indicated the movement of the truck. He said: "You left Bridgeport about twelve fifteen, Barnes." His finger pointed to a gap in the black line. "What was this five-minute stop?"

Bookie leaned over. "I picked up the Lindsay guy there," he explained.

The blunt fingers found another gap. "And what about this second stop a couple of minutes later?"

"That was at the wagon right outside Fairfield when Lindsay was killed. And there," pointed Bookie, "was where I went into a skid and stopped when I saw something was wrong with Lindsay."

"It checks all right," grunted Hallery, "unless you killed Lindsay in Fairfield and *then* went into the lunch wagon for coffee." He stood up. "That's all. When my men finish checking your truck you can leave. We know you're bonded and all that but in case you still feel like fooling around just remember that this will be a federal case."

Hallery left and Bookie Barnes walked outside. Seven or eight men were giving the semi-trailer a going-over. Bookie knew what they were looking for. Narcotics.

A cop came over and said that there was a long-distance phone call waiting. Bookie Barnes went inside and found that it was Mr. Murdock calling him from Washington.

The owner of the trucking concern was nearly unintelligible with excitement. "Bookie, I heard that detective or whatever he was from the narcotics bureau was murdered while you were carrying him. What happened?"

Briefly, Bookie Barnes explained.

"Oh God," moaned Murdock. "As soon as Lindsay came to me this afternoon I flew down here to see if I could do anything. Bookie, do you realize we operate under an I.C.C. charter?"

Bookie Barnes said he realized.

"Well, if the government connects us with drug peddling or blames us for this murder all they have to do is take away our certificate of public convenience and necessity and we're in bankruptcy. Bookie, you're right there—right in the middle of it. Maybe you could find a way out."

"Maybe," admitted Bookie reluctantly. "I've got a vague hunch about this whole thing but the cops don't pay attention."

Mr. Murdock seized at the straw. "Well, for God's sake, follow it up, Bookie. I'll square the cops. You're not a dumb bolix of a driver. You got brains. Get me out of this mess and you can write your own ticket."

"We'll see what happens," said Bookie. He cradled the receiver.

NOTHING OUT of the ordinary had been found on the truck and once more Bookie Barnes was on the ice-coated road. He was hours late already but he didn't worry about the overtime or whether Bill Connelly would pay him for it. He knew that something was brewing, that the greaseball and probably Bushy-brows would be after him again. He knew that he was skating on ice much thinner than that which coated the Boston Post Road.

He passed through Norwalk and as he reached its southern boundary a traffic light stopped him.

"How about a lift, mister?"

Bookie looked out the door window. The voice belonged to a woman. It sounded young and, while he couldn't be sure in the semi-darkness, she looked pretty. Bookie indicated a sticker on his windshield. "Sorry, sister. No riders."

"Mister, you've got to help me." Her voice was urgent, almost hysterical. "My boy friend and I came for a ride down this way from New York and we had a fight and he left me stranded. I have no mad-money on me and you've got to take me back."

"Sorry, sister," he said shortly. "You should get Dorothy Dix to give you a lift."

She jumped on the running board. "Mister, you wouldn't let your own dog out on a night like this."

"I haven't got a dog," said Bookie. "Beat it." He wanted to go ahead but the light had turned green and was now red again.

"Please, mister. I can't get a lift into New York from anybody else and it isn't any Palm Beach out here in this wind."

He could see her lips tremble from the cold and shivering spasms coursed up and down her body under the thin topcoat. "All right," he said reluctantly. "Jump in."

She gave a squeal of delight, went around to the other side and climbed into the cab. He shifted into first and they moved ahead. The girl sighed with relief as she felt the comforting warmth from the motor.

"You're O.K., mister." She peered at him as they passed a lamp light. "You even look O.K. What's that you got under your jacket—a barrel?"

"A spare tire from the truck," said Bookie. "How'd you get stuck? The boy friend get fresh with you?"

"Yes. That's what happened. Can I have a cigarette?"

He extended his package. She took out a cigarette and dropped the package into a pocket of her coat. He didn't take his eyes off the road but said: "Let's have it back."

She laughed ruefully. "My mistake. Times are kind of tough, you know."

He said: "You didn't go out for any ride tonight dressed the way you are. Besides, you had no boy friend to get fresh with you because nobody would try anything right in the middle of the Boston Post Road."

She laughed again. It sounded pleasant to Bookie Barnes, though a little forced. "O.K., Hawkshaw. Besides, if any man got fresh with me *I'd* take the car and *he'd* walk home."

"Then how come you were stranded?"

"I'm a hoofer, mister. Spelled with an 'f.' I went up to Boston with my last cent thinking I might get a spot in a vaudeville house up there but I was too late. So I've been thumbing my way back to New York. Is that better?"

"Much better," said Bookie. "I'm only giving you a ride but I don't feel like being taken for one."

She reached over and squeezed his arm in a friendly fashion. "You're all right, mister. My stage name is Cleo but you stick to Sheila."

"And you can call me Bookie. This is pretty bad weather to be hitch-hiking."

"Especially if you're hungry," Sheila agreed. "Besides, I don't take every ride that comes along. I stopped a truck that looked like this a little while before you came along. The driver was eating a piece of candy but I didn't like the gleam in his eye so I told him to shove off with his scooter."

"That was probably Latch," Bookie said and frowned. Latch should have been pulling into the New York terminal by now. What could have held him up? He remembered that it was Latch who originally started out with David Lindsay. A peculiar thought struck him. He looked sideways at the girl and asked: "Do you know anyone called Lindsay?"

"Lindsay? Is he in show biz?"

"Forget it."

A HAZE had settled over the road and with it Bookie Barnes had the feeling of something inescapable closing in on him. They had left Darien and Stamford behind them and were approaching Greenwich. The girl smoked lazily, her head resting on Bookie's knotted shoulder.

"You're white," said Sheila after a while. "I like you, Bookie."

"I'm just giving you a lift. Don't make it too thick."

"I mean it. You haven't even tried to put your hand on my knee. A girl appreciates that kind of thing."

He grinned. "Maybe I've been too busy worrying about something else, Sheila."

"About what?"

"A murder that—" He broke off as a station wagon pulled up alongside the tractor. He hadn't noticed its approach because it was running without lights. He knew it was the same one that was at the roadside when Bushy-brows had stopped him.

There was a sharp crack and a neat bullet hole appeared in the unbreakable glass.

"God damn them," said Bookie and pushed down on the gas.

The station wagon shot ahead and cut in, stopping dead a hundred feet in front. Two more holes appeared in the windshield. The station wagon blocked the road. Bookie Barnes didn't hesitate. He pressed down to the floorboard and the dozen-odd tons that comprised the number six unit of Murdock Motor Freight plowed on.

The semi-trailer smashed straight into the station wagon. Ordinarily, the car would have folded up like the Tacoma Bridge but as the tractor struck, it gave no resistance on the glassy macadam. It leaped over the slippery, ice-coated road like a goosed antelope and went into a crazy, pinwheel whirl. It spun around, staying upright by some miracle, finally came out of it, lurched ahead and disappeared.

But Bookie Barnes was noticing none of this for, as he hit the station wagon, the dozen tons under his hand shuddered and started swinging, pendulum-like, from one side of the road to the other. It was like the swish of a maddened tiger's tail. Then, slowly, the dizzy arcs it made grew narrower and the pull on the wheel became lighter. Finally, almost resentfully, it gave a last skittish lurch and straightened out.

The semi-trailer rolled on toward Greenwich, a grim-faced Bookie Barnes behind the wheel. He remembered the girl in the cab with him and looked at her.

"How come you didn't scream?" he asked.

"I'm not the type," replied Sheila. "Though I was plenty scared." She took lipstick from her purse and began to write figures on the windshield.

"What are you doing?"

"I managed to get their license number, Bookie. They were New York plates."

"Don't bother," he said. "Those plates are stolen. That was a Connecticut car."

She returned the lipstick to her purse. "What were they, anyway? Hijackers?"

"I know who they were. Just forget it, Sheila."

"All right." She leaned back, then gave a sudden squeal as they passed a building. "Where are we, Bookie?"

"We're nearing Greenwich," Bookie said.

"Of course. No wonder it was familiar. I used to do an act at the Golden Slipper here. Have you ever been at that place?"

He shook his head. "No, but I know where it is. It hasn't got a very good reputation, either."

"But that's only because they sell liquor after hours. Lots of places do it and the people who run the Golden Slipper are very nice. Why don't we drop over there?"

He laughed. "Dressed the way I am in a place like that?"

"But we could drive around the back and have something in the kitchen. They'd do anything for me, Bookie, and I could use a drink after those hijackers. Besides, you've been so awfully white—"

"I don't drink on the job, Sheila."

"We can have coffee then. You drivers always make stops and it isn't much out of your way."

"The Golden Slipper is out," he said flatly. "My regular stop in Greenwich is Delmonico's and I want to check on those plates there."

"You mean that that station wagon came from Connecticut? How could you tell?"

"Did you happen to notice that nickel frame that held those license plates in the back? There was a red circle right in the top centre of the frame."

"What of it?"

"Well, I've seen them before. It's a mark used by a Connecticut car agency around here. Those babies put on phoney plates but they neglected to switch that frame.

"Do you know what car agency that is?"

"Not yet but we may find out here. It gives us something to work on."

They pulled up at a lunch wagon. Four trucks were parked outside—two of the jobs belonging to Murdock. Bookie and Sheila climbed off the cab and went into Delmonico's.

CHAPTER FOUR
FLOOR SHOW

THE TWO drivers from other companies listened as Latch gave a colored version of David Lindsay's refusal to ride with him and Steve Czerno was retelling the story of his fight with the narcotics man.

Bookie Barnes and Sheila sat down and ordered ham and eggs. Bookie sized up the girl with interest as he saw her by light for the first time. His guess had been right. She was definitely something to turn your head after.

"Ah, a woman," said Latch, and sat down next to Sheila. "Lady, how come you let this overgrown collegiate pick you up and you turn down a handsome guy like me?"

"What are you doing here, Latch?" cut in Bookie quietly.

"Just what you and Steve are doing here."

"Steve and I were held up in Norwalk by the cops but you should be in New York by now."

Latch gaped in surprise. "You becoming a company stool, Bookie? I slid into a ditch this side of Westport and was stuck for over an hour. What about it?"

Bookie Barnes tried a shot in the dark. "I don't remember any ditch this side of Westport you could get into."

"Look," said Latch with heat, "I was in that ditch. Did you expect me to bring it along for proof?"

"Forget it." Bookie turned to the others. "Any of you crumbs know an auto agency that uses a red circle for a trade-mark on the frames that hold the plates?"

Baldy, a driver who made a nightly run down to New Jersey, spoke up. "Ask me that one. I bought a car from them."

Bookie Barnes felt a tingle of excitement. "Go on."

"It's an agency right in this town run by a guy named Hank Tanner. They handle a Chrysler line."

"Where does this Tanner figure in anything?" asked Lou Selinski, the fourth driver.

Bookie Barnes said: "I was jumped by a bunch of gorillas a little while ago. They pumped some bullets at me and beat it. I spotted that marking over their phoney plates."

Blank, angry silence greeted Bookie's words. Then Baldy said to Sheila, "Close your ears, lady," and began to swear with a scientific preciseness.

Lou Selinski went out to check and came back in a few moments. "They're bullet holes, all right," he confirmed.

"Guys like that oughta have their bellies kicked right through their backs," muttered Steve Czerno.

"Do you think this Hank Tanner could tell us anything about the car they used?" Bookie asked of Baldy.

"We'll see."

Baldy strode to the wall telephone in a corner and searched in the local telephone book chained to it. He found Tanner's home number and dialed. Several minutes of persistent ringing finally roused the car dealer. The driver reminded Mr. Tanner that he was a customer with a few payments due yet, then turned over the phone to Bookie.

Bookie Barnes said: "I'm trying to track down a car—one that you sold."

"What make?" asked Mr. Tanner's sleepy voice.

"I don't know but it was a station wagon."

Mr. Tanner thought a moment. "Hell, I don't think I can help you on that, I haven't sold a station wagon since last year and that was to one of our local business men."

"Who was that?"

"I forget his name," replied Mr. Tanner. "He's the guy who owns that joint outside of town here. You know—the Golden Slipper. He bought a Plymouth wagon."

"Thanks." Bookie Barnes slowly pronged the receiver and turned around. He didn't look at the girl who sat tensely at the counter. "No luck," he said. He thought he heard a relieved sigh from the girl.

"Hell," said Lou Selinski, "what'll we do about it? We can't just let 'em get away with a thing like this."

"Just leave it to me," replied Bookie. He finally turned to the girl, his lips parted in what he hoped was a smile. "Are you ready, Sheila?"

She nodded, he threw some change on the counter and they went outside.

BOOKIE BARNES helped Sheila into the cab, then snapped his fingers. "I forgot to tell Latch something. I'll be right back."

Bookie went inside the lunch wagon and said to the four drivers: "The next stop is on me. It's my treat. You can order anything you want."

"Don't repeat that," said Baldy, "or we're liable to take you up."

"I mean it, guys. You can even have steaks. The place is the Golden Slipper—only don't take too long getting there."

The drivers stared at Bookie. "He's got delusions of grandeur," Steve Czerno finally said. "He couldn't afford the cover charge at the Golden Slipper."

"Be sure to come," insisted Bookie, "as a favor to me. It's open house."

"The guy's really serious," marveled Lou Selinski.

"You're damned right I am. Don't forget."

Bookie Barnes slammed the wagon's door behind him and returned to the semi-trailer. He started it, moved down the road till he reached the first crossing, then turned right. His face was set in hard lines and his stomach felt as if it were tied into a complicated Boy Scout knot.

"Haven't we gone off the Boston Post Road?" asked Sheila.

"That's right, girlie. I decided to accept your invitation."

"You mean to stop in at the Golden Slipper? What changed your mind so suddenly?"

"Nothing. You said you used to work there, didn't you?"

"Of course."

"Well I'm just accepting your invitation."

"Swell," she said. "I know they'll treat us right."

"You told me I was a great guy to give you a lift, Sheila, and now you've got a chance to repay the favor. Besides, you like me. Don't forget that."

"Of course, Bookie. Only it's strange that—"

"What's strange? I'm just a nice guy. A dumb truck driver who gave you a ride and you like me. Don't you remember?"

"Bookie." Her voice was puzzled. "What's got into you?"

He didn't respond. They had left the town limits of Greenwich and were now traveling down an unpaved road. As they moved deeper in, the road became worse, the houses fewer and it was not long before they halted in front of the Golden Slipper.

The cars parked out front either glittered from a lot of chrome and nickel to prove they were expensive or had a discreet lack of glitter to prove the same thing. The building was large and barnlike and the sign in front was unlit. Even if the owners of the Golden Slipper paid protection, they were careful not to advertise the fact that they stayed open all night.

Bookie Barnes pocketed the truck key, got off and went around to the other side. "All right," he said. "Let's go in."

"But Bookie, not in front here. Let's drive around to the back. You have plenty of room there to park the truck and we can eat in the kitchen."

"Keep your story straight, Sheila. You told me you know them in there. They're friends of yours and they won't mind if we go in the front way. Come on." He lifted her down from the cab. He held her for a moment, bent over and kissed her hard on the lips, then released her.

She stared at him, smiling faintly. "It must be an early spring. How'd it taste?"

"Like kissing Benedict Arnold," he said harshly. "Come on."

THE WEARY hatcheck girl gaped in surprise at the truck driver clad in corduroy pants, aged leather windbreaker, and peaked cap. The club's gladhander, dressed in tuxedo, hurried over and blocked Bookie's path.

"Where do you think you're going?"

"Inside. I'm invited."

"Dust, bum. Dust."

"I don't feel like arguing," said Bookie. He grabbed the gladhander by the side of the arms, lifted him completely off the floor and gently set him aside.

The hatcheck girl said admiringly, "Holy cats," and Bookie and Sheila went inside the club and sat down at a table.

In contrast to the shabby exterior, the inside of the Golden Slipper was all dim lights, paneled walls, hand-woven drapes and a glass, goldfish bar. Up front, a few tables were placed together to accommodate a champagne party that was in its passing-out stage. A few lushes drank at the bar and talked to the goldfish and several deuces were rubbing knees in wall booths. Most of the customers wore evening clothes and if they weren't many they were certainly money.

A waiter came over to Bookie's table and gaped down at him. "What's this? A gag or a masquerade?"

"Neither," replied Bookie Barnes. "We just dropped in for a friendly visit because Sheila's known here. Aren't you, Sheila?"

She smiled nervously at the waiter. "Sure I'm known here. Hello, Tom."

Tom said: "Hello." He had a square, stocky build and probably doubled as a bouncer.

Bookie rubbed his hands together with satisfaction. "Now that's straightened out. I'll have coffee and dough-nuts, Tom. And also eighteen dollars and seventy cents."

"What!"

"You heard right, Thomas. The coffee's for me and the dough is for a new windshield on my truck. I've got a couple of little holes in that windshield and I don't feel like paying for it out of my own pocket."

The waiter's hand clenched and Sheila grabbed his sleeve. "You better go in the kitchen and do as he says, Tom. Bring him what he needs—I mean what he asked for."

Bookie nodded approval. "And bring a sample of some narcotics you probably have around here. Is it opium or morphine or what?"

The waiter glanced at the girl and then headed for the kitchen. Sheila said: "Bookie, you're acting so strange. As if you thought these people were mixed up with those hijackers."

"Take your whiskers off, girlie. I know you. I know damned well that you sent Tom into the kitchen to get help."

"You're crazy!"

"Girlie, if it wasn't that I was so lazy I'd slap you around this upholstered sewer till your teeth rattled."

Tom came from the kitchen followed by two men. They were the greaseball and Bushy-brows. The latter's face was taped where it had been smeared by the searchlight and the greaseball carried coffee and doughnuts which he set before Bookie with an elaborate bow.

"How's that for service?"

The greaseball and Bushy-brows sat down and the waiter moved around to stand close to Bookie Barnes. The gladhander appeared and stood on the other side. Bookie began to sip the coffee.

THE GREASEBALL beamed at Bookie Barnes. "Well, well, if it ain't the gentleman truck driver. I'm glad you dropped in."

"You're glad too soon," replied Bookie. "And don't think I walked into this joint with closed eyes. I knew what I was heading for and I knew why she wanted me here."

Sheila moved away and sat next to Bushy-brows. Her eyes were no longer friendly and her mouth was thin and sneering.

"At any rate, it worked," said the greaseball. He nodded to Bushy-brows. "It was his idea to use sex if we couldn't stop you on the road. And by that lipstick on your puss, Bookie, I guess she used it."

"You lousy tramp," muttered Bushy-brows. "Did you have to neck him?"

Bookie finished the coffee. "O.K.," he said. "Let's have the dough for the windshield and I'm getting out of here."

The gladhander laughed. "He really thinks he's getting out of here."

"What else do you want?" asked the greaseball.

"I want to find out who killed David Lindsay. I want to find out who's the head man around here, what kind of drug running you're mixed up with, and what you want from me, because I'm getting damned sick of being pushed around."

The greaseball became serious. "You got the lay all wrong, Bookie. If you would of come around to the kitchen nicely maybe you would of had coffee and never known what happened. But you're too nosey and things are different now. We're giving and you're taking."

A man came over to the greaseball and whispered into his ear. The greaseball said: "Let's have the key to your truck. We're driving it around to the back."

"I want the dough for that windshield and I want it now."

Sheila pointed. "He put the key into the right-hand pocket of his jacket."

Bookie said: "I'm getting mad and I'm liable to start breaking things. Let's have that money."

The beefy waiter leaned over to extract the key from Bookie's pocket. Bookie didn't move from the chair but his fist shot up and caught the waiter under the chin. The waiter went down like a gallows trap. A couple of drunks started applauding.

The greaseball's lips compressed. He said: "Get them out of here."

Bushy-brows and a couple of waiters made a round of the tables and booths expressing their polite but firm regrets that they were closing down. In two minutes the place was cleared. A couple of more gorillas came out from the kitchen and added to the circle around Bookie's table.

The greaseball tapped with a salt shaker to emphasize his words. "All right, Bookie. You made a crack about Lindsay. Why? How much do you know? You better sing quick if you don't want to be buzzard meat."

Bookie stood up, his eyes gauging the surrounding gorillas and the distance to the door. One of the men moved in closer and he felt a gun jab into the small of his back.

Sheila caught her breath. "But you're not going to—"

"Save it, girlie," interrupted Bookie Barnes.

"Sure," agreed the greaseball. "It's a little too late to give you a break, Bookie. I didn't like that crack about asking us who killed Lindsay. You're finished."

Bookie thought he heard a sound from the outside, then he was sure of it. He grinned. "We got visitors," he said.

THE DOOR to the Golden Slipper opened and Latch, Steve Czerno, Baldy, and Lou Selinski marched in. They sighted Bookie and came over.

"Say, this is swell," said Latch. "We took a chance you weren't kidding us and we came around this way and saw your truck outside. So you've really got an in over here."

"I've got an in, all right," replied Bookie. "In fact, I've got a gun in my back right now."

Lou Selinski laughed heartily. "Bookie, you're terrific."

Baldy strayed over to the bar. "Are those real fish?" he called.

The gorilla with the gun in Bookie's back stepped aside and the drivers saw the weapon. An automatic appeared in the greaseball's well-kept hand.

"Maybe you believe me now," said Bookie.

Lou Selinski's square head went back and forth. "I don't like this," he stated. "Guns are dangerous."

The greaseball smiled. "That's right. He waved the automatic. "Line up, you bums."

"These are the babies that ganged up on me before," said Bookie Barnes. He waited, tensed and ready. He watched the tendons stand out on Selinski's thick neck as the driver became angrier. He knew something had to happen—that one of the drivers would make a break and he didn't intend missing the chance. He watched Lou Selinski make a sudden dive at the nearest gorilla, grab him by pants and collar and hurl him at the greaseball like a crate of oranges.

At the same instant, Bookie whirled on the gorilla holding the gun next to him and his foot kicked out—catching the wrist and sending the weapon skittering over the floor. He dove after it, his heavy bulk knocking aside two of the others.

Bookie stood up with the gun and barked: "Drop it." The gorillas froze and Latch fished out the greaseball's automatic from the tangle of arms and legs.

The greaseball stood up, drew a comb from his breast pocket and began passing it through his ruffled hair. "I guess it's your deal, Bookie," he remarked drily. "What now?"

Lou Selinski said to Bookie Barnes: "I still don't like guns. What do you say?"

Bookie looked at the gorillas. There were ten of them—two for every one truck driver. Bookie shrugged. He had a score to even. "I'm game," he replied and sent the gun in his hand crashing behind the bar. Latch did the same with the automatic.

The gorillas gaped, the greaseball said something about honor and then they confidently waded into the drivers. But suddenly, things began to happen. Sledge-hammer fists exploded in the gorillas' faces and they were grabbed by steel, octopus-like fingers. One after the other, clumsy paws that were used to heavier labor connected with temple, jaw, or neck and the gorillas spread out on the waxed floor like so many sides of beef.

Baldy went into the kitchen and returned with one ball of twine and one Filipino cook. Within a few minutes, gorillas, bartender, waiters, and chef were all securely bound. Steve Czerno rubbed his knuckles. "Now we'll make them talk," he said.

Bookie regarded the dazed gorillas and shook his head. "Let's wait till they get out of it. We can look around first."

The drivers agreed. They retrieved the guns from behind the bar and trooped into the kitchen. They wandered around, poking into Frigidaire, lavatories, dressing-room and office. They began to descend into the basement when Bookie suddenly stopped short. "The chippies!"

"What chippies?" asked Selinski.

"Sheila and that hatcheck girl. Where are they?"

No one seemed to remember and they hurriedly retraced their steps. But it was too late. The only signs of the gorillas were the pieces of string they had been bound with, strewn over the floor. From the outside, came the sound of cars starting up and racing down the driveway.

CHAPTER FIVE
ARRIVAL

THE DRIVERS were drinking from a bottle labeled Clos-Vougeot 1903, and smoking Coronas. Bookie Barnes said, "Then are we agreed? They got away and we can't do anything about it, so we kept quiet. We say nothing to the cops."

"Sure," nodded Baldy. "What could we tell 'em, anyway? We'd just be asking for trouble."

"Fine," said Bookie. "They told me to keep out of it once and they won't feel so good when they find out I loused this job up."

Latch was poking around behind the goldfish bar. "Holy hell! They don't even carry Krisp-Krunches in this dump." He sounded aggrieved.

"Do you always have to eat that garbage?" asked Steve Czerno.

"My blood craves sugar. Why don't we finish looking around this joint?"

They polished off the bottle of Burgundy and descended to the basement. The place served as the Golden Slipper's storehouse. Boxes and crates of provisions, cases of drinks, bags and cans were stacked high everywhere but in one corner.

A modern, six-burner gas stove rested in this corner and a long, wooden table next to it was loaded down with pots, pans and kettles, glass jars and copper tubing. Carolina pine shelves, lining the wall above, sagged under the weight of five-gallon tins and smaller glass, liquid-filled jars. The boys inspected the contents of the tins and readily identified it as pure alcohol. The jars were more of a problem. Bookie went over and examined them.

"These are filled with different kinds of acids," he finally pronounced.

The boys didn't seem impressed.

Bookie walked along the shelf and paused by a small square of paper with some white substance on it. He bent over and whistled. "We've got something here," he said. "It's what I've been looking for. This is heroin."

Baldy examined the crystalline powder with a suspiciously professional air. "It's snow, all right," he affirmed.

Bookie Barnes snapped his fingers. "I have it! This basement is a refining plant. They manufactured heroin here."

"I thought snow was growed," said Steve Czerno.

"Gum opium is," replied Bookie, "and that's the crude drug from which heroin is made. Here they dissolve the gum opium in alcohol and draw it off and treat it with those acids. The result is heroin."

Latch said: "Say, if those gorillas think we might find out about this they'll be coming back here after us with tommy guns."

"I guess we'd better beat it," agreed Bookie.

BALDY, STEVE Czerno, and Lou Selinski, their arms loaded with caviar, anchovies, fifths of Scotch, and boxes of cigars, got into their trucks and hurriedly drove away.

Latch seemed to hesitate, then walked over to Bookie who was getting into his semi-trailer. He said: "What'll you do?"

"About what?" asked Bookie.

"About this whole business. Don't tell me you're going to drop the whole thing right here. It's not like you."

"I don't intend dropping it, Latch. They started it and I'm going to finish it. I'm after their ringleader. And what's more I intend to find out who killed David Lindsay."

"Well, I didn't," Latch pointed out. "I was inside the wagon with you while Lindsay was being killed."

Bookie nodded. "So was that greaseball in the wagon trying to detain me while Lindsay was being killed."

"What the hell are you getting at?" demanded Latch.

"That's all right. I'm just trying to figure how it happened. While I was inside that wagon, someone stole up on Lindsay, yanked the door open and stuck an ice pick in his back because it was a quiet way to do it. It was plenty premeditated and I'm after somebody who knew that Lindsay would be there at that time. Somebody who runs the whole business."

Latch frowned. "I get the point. You figure there must be a connection between this gang and our outfit."

"Of course. Lindsay was riding our truck. He started out with you and then changed his mind because something happened—maybe because he didn't trust you."

"I never saw him before in my life," stated Latch.

"That's in your favor," said Bookie thoughtfully. "Lindsay changed his mind only after you stopped outside of Fairfield to see if you could help Mike Projak out of the ditch. You claim that Lindsay got off at that time, and only when he was getting back on the cab again did he change his mind. He must have realized he was on the wrong cab."

"How? They all look the same."

"The trailers do," replied Bookie, "but not the tractors. They're numbered. He saw the eleven on yours and might have wanted to ride on six which I drew."

"Have you searched your cab?"

"That's just the trouble. The cops did and they found nothing, but I guess we can look again."

The cab didn't look promising. They sounded the walls and top and pulled out the back-rests, but could find nothing. Bookie pried up the floor boards—to see transmission and motor casings and the dirt road below. He pulled out the seat cushions and poked among the assortment of wrenches, hammers, levers, and accessories. Nothing seemed out of the ordinary.

Bookie replaced the cushions. "It doesn't make sense this way," he muttered. "These gorillas stopped me for something on the road and they sent that chippie out to decoy me here. And Lindsay had to be on to something or he wouldn't have been shived."

"The hell with it," said Latch. "I'm getting out before those gorillas come back with mechanized troops." He paused. "And you better not try to hang any kind of rap on me, Bookie." He climbed into the cab of his truck unit and rumbled away.

Bookie got into his own cab, turned the motor over and started off. He followed the dirt road around and felt relieved despite himself when he again picked up the Boston Post Road. The bitter cold had relaxed somewhat and the ice had turned into slush. Above, he could see the first lemon streaks of the rising sun.

He drove automatically, his thoughts reviewing everything in search of some item he might have missed or forgotten. Suddenly, he remembered something. He hadn't seen a spare fire extinguisher under the seat and there was supposed to be one there.

He stopped, pulled up the seat cushions again and regarded the tools. The fire extinguisher was missing but what interested Bookie more was that there wasn't even room for it. He knew what that had to mean. He took out all the tools and examined the bottom. It was fastened down with heavy screws.

Bookie Barnes worked for twenty minutes with a screw driver before the bottom came up—revealing a shallow compartment underneath. It was filled to capacity with small tins—over twenty of them. He took out a tin and opened it. Inside, were a half-dozen, eighth-ounce vials and he didn't have to open any of these small bottles to know that each contained heroin.

This then was why David Lindsay had been killed, why the gorillas had tried to get at the truck for twenty or thirty minutes—just long enough to remove the heroin. Bookie's face was drawn tight. He knew who had murdered David Lindsay.

THE SEMI-TRAILER rolled through the Bronx, across the Harlem River and down First Avenue. Ten minutes later, Bookie Barnes turned into the New York terminal of Murdock Motor Freight.

A sleepy-red-eyed Bill Connelly was there, listening to the story of the night's adventures from Latch and Steve Czerno, who had pulled in with their outfits a short while before. The foreman didn't seem to relish the story.

Jeff, Dutchy, Mike Projak, and other of the Murdock drivers who were waiting to make the return trip to Bridgeport, listened avidly. Also present, was a mild-mannered stranger in a blue serge suit. Bookie guessed him to be a federal man.

The foreman whirled on Bookie. "I heard all about it," he yelled. He stabbed a finger at the semi-trailer. The tractor's front fenders were creased where they had hit the station wagon and bullet holes spotted the windshield.

"A safety driver," commented Connelly witheringly, "with a tin button in his cap to prove it. You need a calendar, not a clock to check your trips." He beckoned a driver. "Bugsy, uncouple this tractor and take it around to the repair shop."

Bookie waved the driver back. "Leave it there."

"What!" yelled the foreman.

"Why are you so anxious to get it out of here?" asked Bookie. "I don't know the current price of heroin, but there's a good many thousands of dollars' worth of it inside the cab. Is that why you want it moved?"

The stranger moved in closer.

"What are you getting at?" demanded Connelly.

Bookie said: "I'm just getting at a neat racket—a way of distributing drugs. Using a trucking concern as a delivery system. Hiding the stuff inside the tractors and sending them to the points where needed. Murdock Freight is perfect for that because we cover the whole eastern seaboard. All you need is a guy at each terminal to take the stuff out."

"Holy mother of hell," said Bill Connelly. "If you think I'm going to listen to any more—"

"I guess we'll listen," put in the mild stranger.

Bookie asked: "Bill, why did you tell me to take number six tractor last night?"

"In case you don't remember, you ——, I'm foreman in this place and it's my business."

"Yes," replied Bookie, "but I asked to take eleven because it had chains, but you claimed it didn't have a trip meter card in it yet. But you sent Latch out with eleven and went right out yourself without having a chance to put a meter card in it." Bookie turned to Latch. "Was there a card in your tractor?"

"Sure was," said Latch. He indicated the stranger. "This egg just checked it."

"Then that's it," said Bookie. "Lindsay must have known Latch would bring in a haul of heroin and went with him. So Connelly switched tractors with a phoney excuse and made me take it instead. Lindsay caught on to the switch when he made that stop outside of Fairfield and changed over to my truck. That was Lindsay's death warrant because he didn't know that Connelly was the gang's distribution head."

"Fairy stories," muttered the foreman hoarsely.

The stranger said: "Shut up, Mr. Connelly."

Bookie continued. "So Connelly got panicky and had some greaseball trail me in the hope they could take the drugs out of the cab. But they had to get rid of Lindsay first so Connelly killed him while the greaseball tried to stall me in the lunch wagon. Only Connelly would know that that lunch wagon was my regular stop and he'd be one guy to have an ice pick in his kit last night because he was up and down the road chasing after accidents."

The foreman was swaying back and forth. "You damned, stinking liar." He made for Bookie Barnes.

They stood toe to toe, hammering at each other with blunt, heavy fists. They threw punches without trying to box or to dodge the other's blow. They hammered away methodically and powerfully as if at a sand bag.

Almost imperceptibly at first, the foreman's blows came more slowly. Then Bookie Barnes was returning two for every one. Suddenly, Connelly's knees buckled and he slipped to the ground.

Bookie leaned against a trailer and fought for breath. After a while, he said to the stranger: "Thanks for not stopping the fight."

"I didn't think you wanted me to, Mr. Barnes."

Bookie Barnes went over to the time clock, fished his card out of the windbreaker pocket and punched it. He wiped some blood off his face, pulled a pencil out of his cap and turned the card over. The pencil poised over the column lettered: *Remarks about trip.*

Bookie hesitated a moment, then wrote: *Delayed by ice—and stuff.*

OVER A BARREL

FAIR EXCHANGE IS NO ROBBERY
BUT—WHEN HIJACKERS LIFTED
36 BARRELS OF FINE HAVANA
TOBACCO FROM BOOKIE BARNES'
BEHEMOTH OF THE HIGHWAY AND
LEFT ONLY A BLOODY CORPSE AS
RECEIPT, BOOKIE LOST NO TIME
IN JOCKEYING HIS JUGGERNAUT
OFF THE POST ROAD AND ONTO
A MURDER ROUTE THAT WOUND
THROUGH A CEMETERY, PAST
A WEDDING PROCESSION, AND
CAME TO A DEAD END IN A NUDIST
CAMP WHERE EVERYTHING WAS
STRIPPED BUT—LUCKILY—THE
GEARS ON BOOKIE'S TEN-TON
BABY.

CHAPTER ONE
TOBACCO ROAD

"**S**VELTE," **WAS** Latch's ecstatic comment on the gorgeous item of fluff that had just entered Carp's Diner. "Strictly for the conny-sewer trade."

"Connoisseur," amended Bookie Barnes who was supposed to know about such things. The boys had dubbed him Bookie because they claimed he read a book before being kicked out of college.

But Latch wasn't listening. He still couldn't get over his surprise at having such an eye-filling bit of femininity walk into the place like any other human being. Carp's Diner just wasn't that kind of joint. It was located on the Boston Post Road where it bypassed Norwalk, Connecticut, and it catered to the truck driving trade. There was no flash about the place, outside or inside, to make anyone want to stop there. The boys called it Ptomaine Ptowers.

Nor was Latch the only one to register astonishment. Pete, the dimwit hashslinger behind the counter, delivered a bleary smile of welcome and began scratching his head in embarrassment. Even all two hundred twenty pounds of Big Dan Carp, owner of the place, stopped in the act of polishing glasses and watched.

And the three ten-dollar millionaires—at least that's how Bookie Barnes had them labeled—at the far end of the counter stopped inhaling their beers and made low-toned comments. They were a hard-looking trio with the natty clothes of their kind. Real sports.

"Oh, hell," moaned Latch disgustedly, "she's convoyed."

Bookie pulled his eyes away from the fluff and saw that a male had come in with her. He just missed being pretty and his nose wrinkled at the smell as if he wasn't used to such places. Newport in summer and quail in winter, decided Bookie, who was in a labeling mood.

The fluff walked up to the counter and spoke to Pete. "I'm looking for a man."

As if on cue, every male grinned to announce his candidacy—especially the three tough-looking sports who dressed it up with low, significant whistles. Bookie Barnes relabeled them, deciding that they were the type who loitered in front of poolrooms trying to spit farther than their companions.

Pete's mouth opened but no sound issued. Pete wasn't exactly a halfwit. Hamburger-happy would be closer. Big Dan Carp, who liked to think he had a kind heart, hired Pete because no one else would.

Big Dan went over and jumped into the breach with his Sunday manners. "May I be of any help, miss?"

"I'm trying to find a man," the fluff repeated. "It's terribly important."

That was probably an understatement, Bookie imagined. The fluff was evidently under some emotional strain. Her hand groped nervously for her handsome escort's arm and those big brown eyes that could melt a Gestapo man's truncheon seemed ready to swim in tears.

"Perhaps if you'd tell me what he looks like or wears—" Big Dan began.

"Yes, of course. He's about thirty-five and he's thin and he's fairly tall—"

"That's me," Latch stage-whispered to Bookie.

"—and he's wearing black and white sport shoes."

"That's not me," Latch had to admit. He looked accusingly at his brogans which were used to pressing truck brakes and clutches.

"I think he's wearing a gray suit," the fluff continued, "and horn-rimmed glasses."

BIG DAN knew very well that no one of that description had been in Carp's Diner that evening but he pursed his lips and appeared to concentrate. "No, miss," he finally said. "I'm sorry but I don't remember anybody like that."

"Are you sure?"

"Yes, miss. Was he supposed to meet you here?"

"Well, he—"

"It's no use, dear," the fluff's escort interrupted. The timing of the interruption didn't seem to be any accident. "I guess we'll have to look some place else."

"I'm afraid you're right. It's no use."

She said it in a way that made every man of them want to rush out and grab his lance and do battle for her.

She thanked Big Dan Carp and left with her escort. For the moment that the door was open, Bookie could see a low, maroon coupé, one of those twelve-cylinder affairs, standing outside. Bookie wondered what urgency could be forcing such a girl to be chasing around truck drivers' joints looking for a man with horn-rimmed glasses and black and white shoes at 12:45 A.M.

Latch ordered a coffee warm-up and became maudlin. "What's wrong with me? Why is it that rich, beautiful dames like that never go for me? We'd get married and she'd tell me to take things easy and when I went to sleep nights she'd stuff ten-dollar bills into my pockets. Why don't such things ever happen to me?"

Bookie Barnes thought of a couple of good reasons but didn't mention them. Big Dan winked at Bookie and Latch and returned to his glass polishing.

One of the sports announced a yen to hear some music. He went over to the juke box, pressed buttons, and pumped change into the machine. The music blared out.

"Louder," called one of the sports.

The first sport, a specimen with a cute dimple on his chin, reached behind the juke box and turned the volume on to its loudest. And that was very loud. The drums of the swing band sounded like an artillery range and the wind instruments like a cyclone tearing through a glass factory.

Big Dan Carp frowned. "Turn that damned thing down!" He had to yell to be heard over the screaming music.

The three sports paid no attention.

"I said turn that lower! You'll wake up Admiral Byrd!" Big Dan set down the glass he was polishing and headed for the blasting juke box.

This time the sports paid attention. They got off their stools and ranged themselves in front of Big Dan, barring his way. They said nothing, just glared at the hash-house owner with cigarettes dangling from their lips, looking their most sinister.

Big Dan, and he was bigger than any of the three, became a pasty white and his hands started to shake. He turned abruptly and walked out of the rear door of the beanery. The sports laughed.

Both Latch and Bookie Barnes swore. They had never imagined that Big Dan Carp had a yellow streak as wide as all that. What made it worse was that Big Dan must have known that the two truckmen would range them-selves on his side.

Pete, the hash-slinger, was only dimly aware of what had happened. However, his eardrums were beginning to ache from the juke box and he crawled out from behind the counter to tone it down. One of the sports stepped up and backslapped him across the face.

Shocked with disbelief rather than pain, Pete stood still. Then his lips began to tremble and he returned to his counter, tail between legs.

Bookie swore again. Ganging up on Big Dan was one thing but slamming around a poor booby-bird like Pete was a little too thick. Before Bookie could decide what to do, Latch stood up and headed for the troublesome juke box.

The sports were waiting.

The first sport let go with an experimental jab, only to catch the full width of Latch's fist in his face. He sat down, quite surprised to find blood running from his nose. A little more respectfully, the other two jumped for the truck driver. Latch didn't wait for introductions but waded into them.

BOOKIE BARNES figured the time was ripe to come to the aid of his profession. Not that Latch needed him. Latch may have looked thin and tubercular and sallow-faced but he was an old truck driver from the wild-cat days and he could handle himself in any free-for-all. But still, Bookie decided, if he did not help, it wouldn't look so good when the story later made the rounds of the wagons on the road.

Bookie sighed and got off the stool. He had a heavy, V-build, steel-hardened by the years of tossing around packing cases and he had a chest like the Goodyear blimp.

The sport with the bleeding nose stood up and launched himself at Bookie, trying for one below the belt. Bookie had to move fast. He sucked in his stomach and his right circled around, catching the sport over an ear and sitting him down again.

Bookie turned to see how his partner was making out. Latch was still holding off the other two though he wasn't having an easy time of it. His lips moved in what obviously were curses but nothing could be heard above the blaring juke box.

Dimple-chin left Latch and braced himself as he saw Bookie coming. Bookie circled to the left to avoid a lashing foot and then closed in. His fist shot out in a short, chopping blow and the sport dropped.

It was heavy and effective and Dimple-chin seemed paralyzed for a long moment. Then he leaped up and at Bookie with redoubled fury. Bookie planted a palm against the sport's chest and the right pulled back. Then he paused.

Bookie felt something over the other's chest—something hard and familiar. His fingers spread out. It was a gun in a shoulder holster. Even as Bookie's right circled to stop right on the dimple he was wondering why the sport hadn't thought of using his gun.

The one with the bleeding nose was back again. Bookie grabbed at his jacket. There it was. Another shoulder holster and no doubt the one who was keeping Latch busy was also packing artillery. Automatically, his mind worrying over the problem, Bookie's fists moved like pistons.

Why didn't the sports try to use their rods?

Latch was being kept busy by his man and the other two kept getting off the floor and rushing at Bookie with blind, hopeful stubbornness. Above it all, continued the ear-breaking obligato of the juke music.

Despite himself, Bookie Barnes felt a grudging admiration for the sports. Perhaps they had thought it would be easy for the three of them to take care of the two truck drivers but now they knew they had met their match—and they still fought like demons. And, for some crazy reason, they weren't drawing their rods.

The one with the bloody nose was now red down to his shirt front and Dimple-chin had one eye closed. Bookie felt a cut over his right cheek but it didn't seem like much. His ham-like fists lashed out, connecting solidly every time, but some deep-rooted urge kept the sports fighting. For the first time, Bookie Barnes wondered if he and Latch would be able to handle them.

The rear door opened and Big Dan Carp stood there, an imposing figure, with an axe in his hand. One of the sports yelled a warning and in another second they had disappeared through the front door, hellbent for their car.

BOOKIE BARNES kicked the plug out of the juke box. The sudden quiet that burst on the place was gratifying. Pete stuck his head up from behind the counter to see if it was safe to come out now and Latch sat down to catch his breath. Bookie fingered his cut cheek and found that the bleeding had already slowed down to a trickle.

Latch finally managed a deep breath and said: "They had more vinegar in them than I thought."

"I don't know. Something's wrong."

"I'm off the beam."

"Those sports," Bookie explained. "How come they were fighting according to Hoyle? They're not the type."

"Hoyle!" snorted Latch. "It was three against two to begin with and practically every punch they tried was below the equator."

"That's just it. They went in for the usual dirty fighting as long as it was small time—but why, for instance, didn't they start throwing things?"

"Say, you're right at that."

"Sure. There were plenty of dishes and sugar bowls and things around. I had my eye on those beer bottles but they never started that kind of stuff and I can't figure it out. It's not because they felt kindly toward us."

"Maybe they were just trying to let off a little steam."

"That's not the way to do it because they got a worse pasting than we did. And how about those rods that every one of them was carrying? Why didn't they pull those when things started going against them?"

This was news to Latch and he frowned, struggling to digest the information. Dan Carp came over to the truck drivers and coughed apologetically to attract attention. The axe was still in his hand and his fingers ran up and down the shaft nervously.

"Look, boys, I'm sorry about running out on you before when those bums showed fight."

"It's all right."

While they still couldn't reconcile themselves to Big Dan's cowardice, Latch and Bookie were feeling somewhat more kindly toward him since he had showed up with the chopper at the right moment. "It ain't all right," Big Dan insisted. "I just don't know what came over me, boys, but—"

"Forget it, Dan. We'll keep it under our hat."

The beanery owner thanked them gratefully and left. If the rest of the drivers ever heard that Big Dan hadn't been around to back up two of them in a fight, they'd boycott the place into rapid and complete bankruptcy.

Latch looked at his watch. "Man, it's after one already and I got a three-hour push ahead."

"What are you carrying?" asked Bookie Barnes.

"I'm taking an empty up to Putman County to pick up stuff in some back-woods warehouse."

The two truck drivers nodded to Pete and Big Dan Carp and went outside. Both of them worked for Murdock Motor Freight, Inc., one of the larger firms covering the New England states and chartered as far south as Pennsylvania.

The two identical semi-trailers were ranged outside of Carp's Diner, huge, menacing monsters in the full moon. Each consisted of the towering trailer—painted a bright, garish yellow like all of Murdock's units—and a powerful tractor to haul it. In his more imaginative moments, Bookie regarded it as some bulldog dragging along a sleek python.

Latch jumped up on the running board of his tractor. "Bookie, are you sure those muggs carried rods?"

"I'm sure."

"Well, what do you know," he marveled.

BOOKIE BARNES climbed into his own cab and turned over the motor. Like a proud mother with her baby carriage, he eased the tractor-trailer combination out of its spot and started on the last leg of his journey to the Bridgeport terminal of Murdock Motor Freight.

It was a warm, balmy night and Bookie Barnes liked driving the trucks in this sort of weather. His windbreaker was on the seat, his sleeves rolled up, his peaked cap pushed far back on his head, and he whistled *Wagon Wheels*. He remembered the gorgeous fluff and hoped she had found her man. He was in a charitable mood.

A stop light blinked in front of him. He pressed down on the brakes and suddenly stopped whistling. The truck had seemed to stop just a little bit too easily, too lightly, for a load as heavy as the one he carried.

Bookie's years of driving had made him highly sensitive to the slightest cough or sneeze in his steel babies. Carefully, he listened to the motor and pumped the brakes. Everything seemed to be working smoothly. Just his imagination, he decided, as he engaged the clutch and moved ahead.

He rolled on, nearing Westport, and took a sharp curve. There it was again! No truck carrying 36 huge barrels of tobacco, weighing 400 pounds apiece, should take a curve as easily as that—not when she was being glued down to the road by a load in excess of seven tons. It was one thing if the truck was acting skittish and having tantrums— you usually knew what was annoying her and a firm hand would calm her down. But this kind of thing was unexpected so it was hard to deal with—and dangerous.

A crazy thought crossed Bookie Barnes's mind. He and Latch might have gotten mixed up and taken the other's outfit. He pulled the emergency and climbed down. No, there had been no such mistake. This was his semi-trailer.

While all of Murdock's newer trailers looked alike and had no identifying mark, the tractors that were coupled to them were numbered. There, on the door of the tractor's cab, Bookie saw the number. Seven. That was his, all right. Latch was shoving number 16 up to Putman County.

Bookie climbed back into the cab and saw other things that proved that he could have made no mistake. There was that nick in the steering wheel and that knob atop the shift rod was still in the shape of a feminine knee as fashioned by some former, waggish driver. All was well.

But Bookie Barnes was still as worried as a piano tuner over a false note he couldn't track down. That silver button pinned to his cap—the badge of a safety driver—was there just because he did worry about seemingly unimportant things. Bookie picked up his flashlight, went around to the back, and threw open the trailer doors.

It was empty.

WEAKLY, BOOKIE BARNES leaned against the tailboard. He had been hijacked of a valuable cargo. But when? And *how?* He had never been absent from the truck long enough for such a job. It takes time—lots of time and sweat and go-carts and men and another truck—to remove 36 barrels of tobacco of that weight and size.

The sports who didn't want to use their rods!

Suddenly, Bookie Barnes divined the answer. He knew why the juke box had been turned up so loud and why they had fought with such time-wasting persistence.

Those sports were part of the hijacking gang. They had picked a fight with Latch and Bookie, inside of Carp's Diner, to keep them busy while their friends were switching trailers on the outside. They hadn't removed the tobacco from the trailer but had simply uncoupled the trailers from the tractors, joining each body to the other truck unit.

Coupling a trailer to a tractor doesn't take long—merely a matter of locking down the supports and connecting the hoses on either side to release the vacuum trailer brakes. Thus the switch was made and Bookie was driving Latch's empty to the Bridgeport terminal while, at this moment, Latch was hauling the tobacco up side roads to Putnam County—no doubt heading into a trap at some quiet spot.

Now it was obvious to Bookie that that juke box had been turned on so loud in order to drown out the noise of the tractors as they were being switched. And those sports hadn't used guns or started throwing bottles because they wanted the truck drivers to be in a condition to keep driving. They had hoped that the trick would not be discovered until Bookie pulled into the Bridgeport terminal and by that time Latch would have been taken care of and the load of tobacco stolen.

Again Bookie Barnes looked into the trailer and saw something dark in back. He jumped up and turned on his flash. It was a man's body and blood from a bullet hole soaked the clothing around the heart.

What had that brown-eyed fluff said? Black and white shoes, horn-rimmed glasses, gray suit. Bookie moved the beam of the flash light closer.

There, on the corpse, were the black and white sport shoes, the horn-rimmed glasses, and the gray suit.

CHAPTER TWO
THE BEARDED LADY

IT WAS a new wrinkle in hijacking—switching trailers and sending the load up another road for an appointment with its hijackers, the body of a murdered man who had no apparent connection with the whole thing, a pair of big brown eyes, surrounded by 110 pounds of beauty, coming out of nowhere to hunt for the murdered one—but none of it seemed to make sense and Bookie Barnes gave it up.

He bent over the body, his fingers feeling inside the jacket, and came up with a slim, tooled leather wallet. Inside it were several bills of various denominations and the usual odds and ends that creep into a man's billfold. The identification card read: *Judson Parrish, Mahopac.*

It meant nothing. He replaced the wallet in its pocket, took a final glance at Judson Parrish's sensitive, vaguely aristocratic face, and returned to the cab. He had to hurry. The three sports—no longer subjects for contempt—were racing toward their escape and Latch was heading for his trap.

Bookie Barnes U-turned the semi-trailer and gathered speed. Mike's Bar and Grill, a few miles back toward Norwalk, was the nearest all night spot where he could get to a phone.

He reached Mike's a short while later and cut the motor. Only one car was parked in front. It was a low maroon job—the one belonging to the cutie, or her escort, who was searching for Judson Parrish. There was no need, as Bookie well knew, to search further.

He entered Mike's and sat down at one end of the bar. Sure enough, on the other side, was the fluff. She seemed more tired and more nervous now and her handsome escort had a consoling arm around her shoulders. At least, it was meant to seem consoling.

Mike, portly and pleasant behind the bar, came over to Bookie and voiced his standard greeting for truck drivers. "Hi, draulic."

"Hello, Mike. A beer."

Mike drew it and shoved it over. Bookie lowered his voice. "What's that dame having, Mike?"

"A Scotch and a good cry."

"That's swell. Do me a favor and pull the under-age gag on her. I've got to know who she is."

Mike circled two fingers to indicate that it was in the bag and walked over to the fluff.

"Pardon me, miss, but I just thought of something."

The fluff looked up. "Yes?"

"If I sell liquor to minors I can get in a bad mess and there've been a lot of inspectors in these parts lately."

"What of it?" It was the escort asking.

"I was just wondering if you were over eighteen, miss."

Under less trying circumstances, Mike's approach would have been very flattering. Even at that, she said: "I'm afraid I look my twenty-three years."

"Sure, miss, but if you had some sort of proof like a driver's license...."

She reached in her purse and held out a card to Mike. He barely seemed to glance at it, thanked her, and returned to Bookie.

Mike bent over the bar with a damp cloth and whispered: "Carol Parrish, Mahopac, New York, and after looking in those orbs I'll probably stab my wife tonight."

"O.K., Mike. Thanks."

Of course, thought Bookie. He should have recognized the similarity in features. She and the murdered man in his truck were brother and sister. He hesitated, wondering whether to put in his call first or to tell Carol Parrish that she need no longer search for her brother Judson.

Bookie Barnes decided on the latter and went over to her. "I think I've found that man you're looking for," he announced bluntly.

Delicate fingers caught at his arm. "Where?"

"What do you know of it?" asked her companion truculently.

"I think you'd better come out and see," Bookie Barnes said.

CAROL PARRISH and her escort stood up. Bookie Barnes led the way to the trailer and threw wide the door. The glare of the neon sign proclaiming Mike's food, cut into the trailer, lighting the interior.

Bookie was ready, waiting to catch her if she dropped. However, she didn't faint. A shudder coursed through her and her hands went to her face, blotting out the sight of the body. He could barely catch the words as she spoke.

"Could you please leave us alone for a moment, just a little while?"

Bookie returned to Mike's. At least he had gained one thing by his bluntness. He knew that Carol Parrish's shock at finding her brother dead was not assumed, that she had not known of it—unless she was a better actress than he imagined.

He went to the wall phone and asked for the Norwalk police. Rapidly, he outlined what had happened.

"What? Another one?" shouted the desk sergeant.

"Has there been more of it?" asked Bookie.

"More? This is the third outfit that's been hijacked from under you blind coots this week."

Bookie whistled. Then this was no small-time bunch. It was some big, well-organized gang operating. The desk sergeant's grating questions cut into his thoughts and Bookie gave what little information he could. Latch was driving number 16 of one of Murdock's easily recognizable units and he had to be headed off, before he ran into the trap that was undoubtedly waiting.

"In case, you don't know, this is a big country, Bookie," snapped the sergeant, who knew him. "Where's Latch going? We'd need an army to block off every road in a fifty mile radius."

"He just said he was going up into Putnam County."

"Putnam County's a big place."

"I know, Sarge. I'll get in touch with the main office and ring you if I find out anything. And see if you can get a line on those three sports who kept Latch and me busy. They're probably using the Post Road to get away. Most likely in a stolen car."

"Stop teaching me my business, Bookie. Sit on that corpse of yours till one of my men gets there." The phone clicked off.

Bookie Barnes dialed again—this time the Bridgeport terminal of Murdock Motor Freight, Inc. As he had feared, he could gain little satisfaction from the night foreman who had come on at twelve. He did not know where Latch had been sent, truck routes were locked into the upstairs office, and the traffic manager was home in bed. The foreman promised to rouse the manager and get the needed information.

Bookie pronged the receiver and turned to find Carol Parrish's good-looking escort standing beside him.

"I'm Henry Daly," he said and proffered a hand.

Bookie took it, supplied his own name, and waited.

"I'd like to know how that body got into your truck."

Bookie noted that the most normal question—who murdered Judson Parrish?—he did not ask. He said: "I was in Carp's Diner when you and Miss Parrish came in looking for that man."

"Yes, I remember."

"When I went outside to my truck the body was in there."

"You mean you were driving an empty truck and you just happened to find the body in there?"

"What difference does it make?" asked Bookie.

"I'm a friend of Miss Parrish's and—"

"I mean what difference does it make whether my truck was empty or not. Did you expect me to be carrying a load?"

HENRY DALY'S face reddened. "It's just that I'm naturally interested in finding out the details of the whole thing."

It sounded lame to Bookie but he let it pass. "I was carrying a load but trailers were switched on me."

"I see. Thank you. I'll return to Miss Parrish now."

"Let's make it a trade last," said Bookie. "What did you two do when you walked out of Carp's joint?"

"Why, we just went down the road a little bit to that small gas station nearby and Miss Parrish got out of the car to make a phone call and then—"

"Was it a long distance call?"

"Yes. To New York. But what difference does it make?"

"Then it took a long time."

"Of course, but I don't understand why—"

"I'm just interested in your alibi," said Bookie evenly. "A man was murdered during that phone call."

"Are you crazy?"

"And if she was in the gas station taking a long time about her phone call you could easily have walked back to Carp's and had a hand in the killing. That's why I'm interested."

Henry Daly's lips drew back in a fighting snarl, his head lowered, and his shoulders hunched. A natural fighter's stance, Bookie Barnes automatically noted. Probably an intercollegiate boxing champion in his day—and slick enough not to get marked up.

Bookie had not moved and his long, muscled arms still hung loosely at his sides. However, he presented such a picture of competence that Henry Daly changed his mind. Without speaking, he turned abruptly and walked out to rejoin Carol Parrish by her brother's corpse.

Bookie Barnes phoned Murdock's night foreman again but there was still no news from the traffic manager. He sat down at the bar and Mike came over to put a top on his beer which had gone flat.

"That store window dummy been giving you trouble, Bookie?"

"Just enough to keep it exciting. Ever seen him before?"

"Naw. He come in here a little while ago with the dream-dame and they started asking if I seen someone else. What's this all about anyway, Bookie? What's cooking?"

"Outside of being hijacked and a murder—nothing."

Mike roared. He thought it was good enough to give Bookie a beer on the house. The door opened to admit Uffert, a motorcycle cop attached to Norwalk, who had a genius for picking up stolen cars on the Post Road.

"Hey, Bookie, what's this business you're giving us about a murder?"

Mike stopped roaring. For some mysterious reason, he seemed insulted and he withdrew the beer on the house.

"I found the body after trailers were switched on me," Bookie responded.

"Hmmm. Is that a fact?" Uffert sounded sarcastic. "And what else did you find?"

"Nothing. Those two people outside with the body can probably tell you more."

"Now we've got two live people in addition to one dead one," murmured Uffert. "How nice."

Bookie Barnes became irritated. "Why don't you speak to them yourself and stop giving me the finger?" He strode to the door and stepped out.

There was no sign of Carol Parrish or Henry Daly or their car or even of any body beyond the wide-open trailer doors.

"How very nice," repeated Uffert.

FLASHLIGHT IN hand, Uffert examined every square inch of the trailer floor. "I think your imagination got the better of you, Bookie," he finally announced.

"Listen, Uffert, you know me and you know damned well I don't go off the deep end. I tell you there was a body in here with a bullet in its heart." Bookie Barnes was angry not with the policeman but with himself. He should have kept an eye on the body.

"All right, Bookie, I heard that before but there isn't even any sign of the stiff that was supposed to be in here."

"Did you expect him to carve his name in the floor? He was lying on his back and what blood there was, was soaked up by his clothes."

"And are you quite sure you didn't get the names of the body and that man and woman who are supposed to have stolen it?"

Bookie Barnes thought of the soulful brown eyes floating around in a lake of tears, of the hope and dread in Carol Parrish's voice as she had asked for her brother, and, almost without knowing why, he said: "I'm sure."

They got down from the trailer. Uffert took out pad and pencil. "Now let's get this clear, Bookie. According to you, there are three outfits we're supposed to put a stop-call on. The first is Latch who's romping around with his scooter, God knows where."

"Up toward Putnam County."

"The second are these gorillas who held you off while trailers were being switched. Those two we already know about and the new bunch we're supposed to look for is this man and woman taking a corpse to their glue factory."

"That's about it."

Uffert got on his motorcycle and chugged away without bothering to tell Bookie to hang around and keep in touch with them. He knew Bookie and knew that he was bonded.

Bookie Barnes closed the trailer doors, got into the tractor, and started back toward Norwalk. The brown eyes, the sports, the bullet-pierced heart—none worried him as much as Latch. Perhaps, at this very moment, Latch was being chopped down for a few dozen barrels of pure Havana tobacco. Bookie had sounded the alarm, had done what he could, but still felt vaguely responsible.

The semi-trailer came abreast of Carp's Diner and Bookie parked. Maybe he had overlooked something, perhaps Carp had heard of some new development.

Big Dan sat moodily in a corner of his beanery, nervously running his palms up and down his knees.

"What's eating you?" asked Bookie.

"I can't get over it, how I let you boys down in that fight. If only there was some way I could make it up to you."

The big man seemed genuinely sorry.

"We told you to forget it, Dan. I once opened the wrong door and I was chased three miles by a half-pint husband. Have you heard anything new from those sports or Latch?"

"No."

Bookie strode over to the pay phone and rang the Murdock Freight Terminal again. This time the night foreman had news from the traffic manager.

"We finally woke up the guy, Bookie, and he remembered where he sent Latch. Up to a town in Putnam County."

"Man, I know that but what town?"

"A warehouse supposed to be in a place called Mahopac."

BOOKIE BARNES almost felt like laughing. That's where Judson and Carol Parrish came from and he had never thought of checking to see in what county it was. At last, things were beginning to connect.

The night foreman was saying: "What's doing, Bookie? We got in touch with Old Man Murdock and he nearly blew his top. He claims if we don't get that tobacco back they'll raise the insurance rates on us."

"The hell with his insurance rates. I'm worried about Latch." Bookie replaced the receiver.

He curbed his first instinct to ring the police and turn over the information. It was too late to do Latch any practical good. Either the police had managed to catch up with Latch or, by now, the hijackers had caught up with him. Besides, with the police poking around Mahopac they were bound, sooner or later, to find out about the death of Judson Parrish—and of Bookie's knowledge of it. And Carol Parrish's brown eyes were still there, pleading with Bookie not to involve her. Damn them, anyway.

Bookie arrived at a decision and turned to Big Dan. "You can have your chance to make it up with me, Dan. Come on."

"Swell. Where we going?"

"Putnam County—after some friends of those three sports."

Big Dan left instructions with Pete, his dimwit hashslinger, they went out to the semi-trailer, and got going.

Tersely, Bookie told of the murder and what few items Big Dan did not know.

Watching for the road markers to turn off the Post Road and head for Mahopac, Bookie hardly noticed the cluster of cars and motorcycles at the side of the road till he was nearly upon them. It was a police trap and Bookie pulled over.

Uffert was there, astride his motorcycle, and Sergeant Crawly, who headed the detachment, called out: "You're just in time, Bookie. We're getting the first batch."

"Who?"

"The three of them."

"Which three?"

"The hoods that ganged up on you and Latch at Carp's."

Bookie felt relieved it wasn't Carol Parrish. He asked: "Are you sure it's them?"

Sergeant Crawly broke his revolver and slipped a cartridge into the empty chamber that had faced the trigger. "Dead sure," he said. "They were speeding past Bridgeport, headed for New Haven at a seventy mile clip and a prowl car picked them up and gave chase. They have guts, too."

Bookie felt his sore cheek. "I know."

"They turned right around on two wheels, shot a tire out of the prowl car, sailed back through Bridgeport again, and they're headed this way. They should be showing up here in a half-hour or a little more if they take it easy."

Sergeant Crawly sent a couple of motorcycle cops to the opposite side of the road, to wait there, motors running. Others ranged themselves behind Bookie's semi-trailer, grateful for the covering.

"They're carrying a Thompson sub," Uffert explained.

"Have you got a spare gun?" asked Bookie.

One was passed him and he slipped it into his pocket. As a driver of valuable cargoes, he was licensed to carry one but he had never before done so.

They waited silently, smoking cigarettes with quick, nervous puffs and scanning the cars that passed, A couple of trucks rumbled by, a milk wagon, a few passenger cars with early workers headed for New York, a rattletrap loaded with sleepy-eyed college boys coming down from Yale. The gleaming headlamps that bore down on them did not appear often. Bookie checked his watch. It was well after three o'clock.

"They should be along soon." Uffert's voice sounded discordant and out of place.

"I'd like to get my hands on them," said Big Dan. "That's all I ask."

More cars went by. One of Murdock's semi-trailers, heavy with pipe castings, a drunk who was stopped and taken to the station by one of the men, a speeding newspaper delivery wagon, a sedan bedecked with ribbons, a "Just Married" sign, and with the bride's veil streaming white from the car window. They could hear the noisy rattle of tin cans tied to the rear bumper for many minutes. It was a strange note in their grim task and the sergeant hoped they were sober.

An hour passed, dawn began to break over the horizon, but there was still no sign of the hoods.

Wearily, Sergeant Crawly cracked his limbs as he stretched them. "I guess they turned back or headed down some side road."

Uffert who was now sitting in a prowl car, listening to radio bulletins, let out a yell and ran over. "Those —— got by us!"

"The hell they did," snapped the sergeant. "I know every bus that went past here."

"It was that damned 'Just Married' car with the tin cans! I just heard the report they stopped by a gas station a few miles down and the 'bride' slugged the gas jockey when he got to wondering why she had a two day beard!"

CHAPTER THREE
GARDEN OF EDEN

B IG DAN CARP and Bookie Barnes finished their early breakfast, returned to the semi-trailer, and resumed their journey in the direction of Mahopac.

Now, Bookie felt, he was in the thing to his neck and he had to go through with it. It was too late to give the police the information he had held back and, even if he did, it was too late to do Latch any good. Murdock's number 16 unit hadn't been heard from.

These hijackers weren't beginners. Three truckloads had been spirited away successfully within one week, the gang was big and their timing and teamwork perfect, and they were equipped even down to bridal veils and "Just Married" signs for getaways. Bookie felt it a hopeless job unless he succeeded in finding Judson Parrish's body and the two who had kidnapped it.

Bookie Barnes did not follow the shortest route. Working hunches, which did not materialize, he followed circuitous roads, stopping often to ask if anyone had noticed one of Murdock's trucks pass by there early that morning. No one had and it was nearing noon when they saw a road marker indicating that Mahopac was some nine miles distant.

Big Dan was glum. He had expected more action than being bounced around for hours, stopping only to ask futile questions. "It's like looking for a needle in a haystack, Bookie. We ought to call in the cops."

Gingerly, Bookie Barnes eased the semi-trailer over a bridge that had a five-ton weight limit and merely said: "Maybe."

They were still some miles from the town when they saw a funeral procession approach and Bookie pulled over to let them pass.

Big Dan suddenly bolted up straight. "There's the nifty!"

Bookie looked. In the first car following the hearse, dressed in black, was Carol Parrish. Beside her, still in the comforting business, was Henry Daly. Neither seemed to notice the truck parked by the road and, slowly, the seven or eight cars in the procession went by them.

"I'll bet that's her brother she's giving a quickie burial," Big Dan said.

Bookie nodded agreement. There was hardly any doubt of that. He could guess what had happened. They had brought the body home, had gotten the family physician to issue a death certificate for something like heart failure, and had then decided on an immediate burial.

But it wouldn't do them any good, Bookie Barnes thought grimly. Brown eyes or not, he now knew where the body was and he'd get it exhumed as soon as he could ring the police. The post mortem would have no trouble showing up the bullet hole in Judson Parrish's heart.

"What next?" asked the beanery owner.

The funeral procession was several hundred feet away by now. Bookie Barnes worked the semi-trailer around and began to follow. He said: "We'll find out what connection Judson Parrish had with the hijacking business, why he was killed, and why his sister is giving him a hurry-up funeral without first trying to find out who murdered him."

"And suppose you don't find out."

"Then the cops'll borrow a couple of shovels from the W.P.A. and start digging."

THE FUNERAL procession wound through narrow lanes and it was twenty minutes before they reached the burial grounds.

Bookie Barnes stopped his truck and watched the cars wind through the wide gates—which were purely ornamental as no wall or fence circled the large cemetery—and stop at one of the squat buildings near the center of the grounds. The coffin was removed from the hearse and the mourners followed it inside the building.

"Do we go in after them?" asked Big Dan.

"No. They're probably in the chapel—reading services. Let's wait till they think they've got him safely salted away."

"Think the cutie and her boy friend put the grease under Judson Parrish?" Dan said.

"I don't know what to think, Dan. They're the only clue we have as to where Latch might be and we've got to find him first."

They waited for the reappearance of the casket and the march to the burial plot. Bookie was becoming impatient. His eyes were still on that door a couple of hundred yards away when he felt Big Dan's fingers on his arm.

"Look!"

For the first time Bookie Barnes noticed, through a grove of trees, a road not far from the one they were on, leading to the cemetery grounds. A car had just stopped there and a man alighted and started walking by graves and crypts toward the buildings. It was—beyond any doubt—Bookie's old friend Dimple-chin.

"I guess Latch did head up this way after all," said Bookie. "We'd better see what's brewing."

He and Big Dan got down from the cab and started trailing Dimple-chin. Prompted by some instinct, the gangster's head turned. Surprise stopped him for a moment, then his step quickened. Bookie and Big Dan started to run.

Dimple-puss circled around some monuments, erected to the glorification of people who were probably better off dead, and was out of their sight. They ran ahead but could not find him. By now, they were near the buildings in the center of the grounds.

From the road, they heard a starter turning over. The hijacker had doubled back to his car. There were two derisive toots of the horn and he was gone.

Big Dan emitted a sputtering sound, torn between a desire to curse and the sedative effects of the surroundings.

Bookie laughed tonelessly. "You'd better get back to the truck and sit on it, Dan, before they get that, too."

The hash-house owner left and Bookie made for the building into which the funeral procession had gone. He approached it by the side where he could see French windows, conveniently low. He heard a dry crackle and looked inside, past the drapes. Silently, heads bowed, the mourners were standing around something. One of the men moved and Bookie saw what it was.

It was a crematory!

DESPERATELY, BOOKIE BARNES'S mind whirled looking for some out, some way to get through this blind alley. It was the perfect murder. A normal death certificate and the cremation had fixed it. Now there could be no way to prove his story of the murder. Now he'd just be inviting trouble by going to the police with the full story. The one, the only final proof of his claims was in ashes, behind a conspiracy of silence. It was all very clever. Bookie's face darkened. Everyone connected with the murder and hijacking was being too damned clever. He had been outsmarted all along the line.

The cremation was over. The few men and women who had attended, came out with somber faces and returned to their cars. At the end of the line were Carol Parrish and her friend, Henry Daly.

Bookie stepped forward. "Miss Parrish."

She stopped, turning toward him, surveying him from head to foot as if she had never met him. "Yes?"

"I suppose you're surprised to see me."

She frowned. "I'm afraid I don't remember you."

It was the obvious course. They would deny completely ever knowing him and he could do nothing about it. He was able to look at those eyes and that small, white, oval face without feeling any softening. Bluntly, he asked: "Don't you give a hoot who murdered your brother?"

"This man must be deranged," said Henry Daly smoothly. "Go to your car, dear. I'll take care of him and hand him over to the authorities."

Bookie laughed harshly. Landing in the observation ward of a hospital would be just the right touch.

"Wait, Henry," she said. "Let's hear him out first." She turned to Bookie. "What is it you have to say?"

"Do you deny running up and down the Boston Post Road last night, looking for your brother?" he demanded.

"I was there but what of it? Is there anything criminal in that?"

"Do you deny seeing me, talking to me?"

"I'm not sure. Perhaps. I happened to be upset last night."

"So that's how it is, Miss Parrish. Pretty slick."

"Yes," she said evenly and with meaning, "I'm afraid that's exactly the way it will have to be."

"Haven't you stopped to think that the murderer is still loose, that he's free to kill again?"

"I don't understand."

"No," said Bookie Barnes harshly. "I guess you don't want to. Maybe you don't want to because it was you who held the gun and those angel-eyes that sighted along the barrel before the bullet made a pulpy mess of your brother's heart."

Bookie Barnes could almost hear the horror that constricted her body. Wordlessly, she left him and entered the waiting car. Henry Daly beckoned and stepped around the side of the building. Bookie followed.

"There are a couple of things I don't like about you," Daly stated without preamble. "In the first place, I don't like the underhanded way you learned Miss Parrish's name. I realized it last night after that business about her being a minor but I said nothing."

Bookie regarded the man with amazement. "You don't like it! I'm the one who's in the soup. I reported a murder there's no chance of proving. So you don't like it!"

Daly pursued his point. "In the second place I'm not going to stand for the way you talk to Miss Parrish about the murder of her brother."

"Then you admit he was murdered."

"Yes, but neither you nor anyone else can prove it now. Start anything and you'll be locked up. In the meantime, I'm going to teach you a lesson."

Without warning, Henry Daly uncorked a slashing right. Bookie's original guess had been right. It was the blow of a practiced, expert boxer.

Bookie Barnes, however, had been expecting it. He ducked easily, sank a light left hook in the pit of Daly's stomach, then his right crashed straight forward for six inches, landing flush on the mouth. All of Bookie's disgust and desperation had gone into the blow and the crack of teeth under the impact was a sweet and happy sound to him.

His mouth a fountain of blood, Henry Daly stood up dazedly and staggered toward the dreary sedan supplied by the funeral parlor.

BOOKIE BARNES returned to the semi-trailer. His replies to Big Dan's questions, as they rode back over their tracks, were curt and uncommunicative.

Bookie was wondering about the next move. The murder of Judson Parrish seemed pretty much of a dead end. Latch and the truckload of tobacco was the only trail left to follow. Latch and the truck were some place—probably some place nearby—but where? What had that cop said? This country was a big place.

Down the road, Bookie sighted a figure, thumb extended, asking for a ride. As they came nearer, he could see it was an old woman—proudly, serenely old, with a complete contempt for the subterfuges of cosmetics.

Bookie, who was in no mood for hitchhikers, tried to pass her but she jumped in the middle of the road, directly in front of the tractor. He jammed his brakes. Blandly, completely unaware that a delayed reaction on the part of the driver would have ground her underneath, she smiled, climbed up into the cab, and sat down beside Big Dan.

"Thank you so much for offering me a ride, young man." Her voice was mild and there was a sweet, angelic quality about her.

Viciously, Bookie kicked the great gear shift into first. "I didn't offer anything. My choice was to give you a ride or run you over."

"That's one of the many advantages of being over eighty," she said sweetly. "I can get away with murder."

Big Dan thought of something to say but changed his mind. Bookie asked: "Where do you want to be put down?"

"My, but we're unchivalrous, young man. Turn to the left there and go toward town. And on the way you can tell me what you were saying to Carol by the crematory. When you're finished with that you may tell me why you rearranged Henry Daly's teeth."

More cleverness, thought Bookie Barnes. He should have recognized that dangerous angelic quality by this time. This was Carol Parrish's grandmother.

"Well, young man?"

"I was asking your granddaughter," Bookie said, "whether or not she was interested in finding out who murdered her brother."

The wrinkles on old Mrs. Parrish's face remained serene and unchanged. "And what did Carol reply to that?"

Big Dan and Bookie looked at each other. "They're all nuts," commented the hash-house owner.

"She didn't seem very interested," said Bookie. "Neither do you, for that matter."

"It's just that the Parrishes have guts, young man. That aloof quality. Frankly, it bores me but I follow through. But how do you know Judson was killed?"

"I saw the bullet hole in the heart."

"A good reason. Who do you think murdered him?"

"I don't know yet. It might be your friend, Henry Daly."

The old woman's lips pursed as she considered it. "Perhaps, but I doubt it. He's a little bit too stuffy. His grammar's always so perfect."

"Maybe you know who did it," suggested Big Dan. "Someone whose grammar stinks."

"I do not," retorted the old woman. "What are you two doing here, anyway, chasing after funerals with this monster?"

"What about you?" parried Bookie. "Stop hiding behind your age and tell me about Judson Parrish."

"What would you want to know?"

"To begin with, what connection he had with hijackers, why his body lay in the trailer in place of a load of tobacco."

"Riddles, young man! Would you kindly tell me what you're talking about?"

Bookie sensed that his words were understood only too clearly by the ancient Mrs. Parrish. He said frankly: "I'm in a bad spot. Why don't we let our hair down and swap what we know? I'd be helping myself and you might avenge your grandson's murder."

"I'm sorry," she said, "but I'd rather not. I'll be getting off here."

Bookie Barnes stopped the semi-trailer. They were on the outskirts of the town. The nearest house was a block away, a large, white building, with a picket fence. Next to the garage, Bookie could see another building, certainly large enough to conceal one of Murdock's semi-trailers.

"The Parrish homestead?" he asked.

"Yes." Her eyes followed his. "That place next to the garage used to be Judson's laboratory."

She stepped from the cab and walked down the block.

AGAIN, BOOKIE BARNES had that feeling of helplessness, that sense of having been on the verge of the solution and then missing completely. He and Big Dan Carp sat in the tractor's cab, watching the Parrish home and considering their next move.

A voice said: "What are you doing around here?"

They looked down to see a large man with a shiny badge on his chest and a gun on his hip. A county sheriff of the old, competent, rustic type.

"We're lost," Bookie thought it politic to reply.

"Is that a fact?" The sheriff sounded dubious. "How'd you get here? Which way?"

"Around that way," pointed Bookie, avoiding mention of the cemetery.

"I see. Did you come across that little bridge back there?"

Bookie remembered it. "Yes."

"Well now, that's just too bad," said the sheriff with satisfaction, "because you're coming down to the station with me."

"Why?"

"That bridge has a five-ton load limit on it and I'm getting mighty sick and tired of you fellas coming in here like you owned the place and paying no attention to signs. Aberthnay told me he saw another truck like yourn go over that bridge early this morning and I'm going to put a stop to it."

Another truck! That had to be Latch's. It was the first real indication that Latch was in these parts and Bookie had no intention of spending the next thirty days in jail— or sixty if the judge's sinus was bothering him again.

Bookie switched the key and started the motor. He said: "Call off the dogs, officer. I'll be a good boy."

With magical speed, the gun appeared in the sheriff's hand. It was plain he was no beginner. "Get off that truck, you two!"

Bookie Barnes and Big Dan stepped down. The sheriff reached over and fanned them, removing the gun from Bookie's pocket.

"So you're carrying deadly weapons! You're in for it."

"Listen, officer," pleaded Bookie urgently, "I'm licensed for that and I've got to go some place. I can't afford to be booked on that trick bridge of yours."

The sheriff was unimpressed. Bookie wondered if it was worth grabbing for the rod. Big Dan must have had a similar idea for, suddenly, he lunged.

The revolver spat but Big Dan was moving fast and the shot went wild. Big Dan's square fist smashed against the sheriff's jaw and he crumpled.

For a long moment, they waited. There were no shouts and no sign of commotion. All seemed quiet in the lone Parrish house down the block. Bookie bent over the officer. Heartbeat was all right. He picked up the guns, gave one to Big Dan, and dragged the unconscious figure behind a clump of bushes. They got back to the semi-trailer and rapidly rolled away.

BOOKIE FOLLOWED the narrow side roads and soon found the small bridge. It was about nine miles from Mahopac. Bookie doubted if the hijackers would chance taking the truck through the town and since the vehicle had been seen crossing this bridge it was probably somewhere in between those two points.

Hurriedly knowing that an alarm would be out for them as soon as the sheriff regained consciousness, Bookie worked his way back toward the town. In the next couple of miles they passed nothing but open farm land and a small hut that was boarded-up and empty. They reached a small side road and Bookie turned down it.

"Another hunch?" asked Big Dan.

"More than that. We're getting too near town—closer than they'd chance hiding the truck. They might have turned off here."

They bounced along for another couple of miles over a rutted dirt road, then Bookie stopped. They were in front of some sort of large, wooded estate enclosed by a seven foot anchor fence. Trees and thick foliage made it impossible to look inside. A sign over the front gate read: *Camp Verde*.

Bookie climbed down. "Wait here, Dan. "If I'm not out right away you'd better come in soon because I think we're getting hot."

He walked down the broad, winding driveway and found himself in front of a large, shingled house. He knocked. There was no response and he opened the door.

He found himself in what had been originally intended for the living-room but which had been converted into an office. A desk, chairs, sofa, and some book-shelves comprised the furnishings.

A handsome woman in her late twenties entered by one of the side doors. She wore wedge-heel shoes and a floppy straw hat. She wore nothing between the two.

She said, automatically, "Why, you're dressed," then shrieked and dived behind the desk.

Bookie Barnes grinned.

"Turn around! Please," came the voice from behind the desk.

A gentleman at heart, Bookie did so. Over the entrance doorway a sign asked: *Were Adam And Eve Ashamed?*

"What do you know!" chuckled Bookie. "I've fallen into a nudist colony!"

"Yes, of course," came the velvety voice behind him. "I first thought you were one of us. Who are you?"

"Bookie Barnes. And you?"

"My name is Lora Rawling but that's not what I meant. What do you want?" She still sounded frightened, still seemed to resent the grin she guessed was on Bookie's pan.

"I'm looking for a truck—a truckload of tobacco that was stolen from me."

"Why should you think we have it?"

"It has to be some place around here. Maybe one of you saw it pass while flitting around collecting mosquito bites."

"Mr. Barnes, you speak out of an ignorance of our true nature and purpose."

"Forget it," said Bookie. "If you're sure you haven't seen any truck, I'll run along."

"Not on your tintype." Lora Rawling's voice was less velvety this time and sounded very close to Bookie.

Then, with a sudden ferocity, there was a crashing, blinding flash as something smashed heavily against the back of Bookie Barnes' head.

CHAPTER FOUR
THE SERPENTS

BOOKIE BARNES did not return to consciousness suddenly but gradually and each gradation seemed to specialize in its own particular brand of torture. And he thought that the brands were worth copyrighting.

At first, he was aware of a white-hot poker that jumped playfully over his brain as if plucking harp strings, then this gradually gave way to crushing boulders that dropped on him without warning like so many gigantic ping-pong balls, and this finally fused into a steady, rhythmic pounding inside his head that was less gaudy but quite as effective.

It was in this last stage that his brain started to function and he began to remember what the barroom brawl in back of his forehead was all about.

He has discovered the hiding place of the hijackers with a vengeance—in a nudist colony. The setup was certainly a natural.

If any suspicious character happened on the place, he was confronted by that woman dressed in skin. What had she said her name was? Lora Rawling. She then screamed and got the intruder to turn around and if he remained suspicious she caressed his dome with a wrench or hammer.

A handy thing to have around—that Lora Rawling. A convenient decoy for welcoming visitors. They'd be able to get the drop on a dozen cops with that peep-show system. Unless they were blind or senile. But the hijackers were still being clever. They probably stayed awake nights figuring out these things. Being clever was a good idea, Bookie thought bitterly—so good that it was time he tried it for himself.

Bookie hadn't moved while his mind struggled out of its blankness. Indeed, it was doubtful if he could have moved had he had any desire to do so. Now, he waited for the dull pounding to relent a bit and opened his eyes.

He lay on a sofa in a pleasant room—probably one of the upstairs ones of the house—and seated not far away was Big Dan Carp with a white bandage around his head. That's right. He had told Big Dan to follow him in if he didn't show up and the beanery owner had evidently received the same lethal treatment from that one-woman burlesque show.

Bookie's hand went to his own head and he found a similar bandage around it. He turned and saw what was keeping Big Dan so quiet. Dimple-chin lolled against the doorway, gun in hand. Next to him were two of his strong-arm lads.

"Where am I?" asked Bookie.

"Just give yourself another minute," said Dimple-puss, "and you'll remember."

"What happened?"

"You were bopped by a nudie-cutie," supplied Big Dan Carp with a vast disgust. "Like me."

Bookie Barnes looked at him blankly. "Who are you?"

The hash-house owner blinked. "Don't you know?"

Bookie gave the appearance of studying him. "I'm sorry but I can't remember meeting you before."

"What's all this double-talk?" asked Dimple-chin suspiciously.

"Lora musta bopped him too hard, chief," observed one of the hoods. "He got a dose of amnesia. He's sap-simple."

Maybe there was something to this business of being clever, thought Bookie. He rolled over on his side and, as he had expected, could not find the pressure of the revolver in his pocket. He said: "I guess I must have been in an accident."

"The main accident is still coming," chuckled a hood.

Bookie ignored him though he knew only too well what he meant. "I can't remember things very clearly but I suppose you gentlemen helped me and I want to thank you."

The hoods laughed. Big Dan said: "Snap out of it, Bookie."

"What did you call me?"

"Bookie! Bookie Barnes!"

"Is that my name?"

BIG DAN snorted and didn't bother to reply. Dimple-chin had a whispered consultation with his aides and the three of them left the room. Bookie got off the sofa and walked over to the window. It was a second-story room and he saw it was already dark outside. He could see large, dark shapes looming over the grounds of the spurious nudist colony. The semi-trailers and the hijacked goods were probably in there.

"I can see what you're getting at, Bookie," said Big Dan, "but I think these babies are too smart to be taken in."

Bookie remembered the whisperings of the hoods and decided not to take any chances on a peep-hole in the ceiling or a hidden dictaphone. "Why should they be taken in?" he asked.

"Say, are you on the level?"

Bookie asked him what he meant and Big Dan threw up his hands. The door opened and one of the hoods came in. He jerked a thumb at Big Dan.

"You. Come on."

Big Dan walked out, the door closed. Bookie thought of looking around but went back to the sofa. There was a chance that he was still being watched and, in addition, his head was still being temperamental and it was good to lie down. He wondered if he'd ever see Big Dan again.

In a little while, a hood came with two soggy sandwiches and a cup of tepid coffee. After watching Bookie complete the meal in silence, he asked: "Don't you remember nothing yet?"

"No."

The hood remarked that he was as crazy as a coot and left. It was another hour before he returned and led Bookie to another room. Dimple-chin was there.

"How do you feel, Barnes?"

"Better, thank you. Is that really my name?"

"Uh-huh. By the way, Barnes," said Dimple-chin casually, "I just had a talk with Dan Carp, that friend of yours."

"You mean the big guy?"

"Yeah. I asked him a lot of questions and I suppose you know what they were about."

Bookie pretended to concentrate, then shook his head.

"They were all kinds of questions about the shams, Barnes. Now, you don't know what answers he give me so you're stuck. Get it? Now I'll ask you about the cops and your answers better mesh with Dan Carp's."

So that was the rub! At last Bookie Barnes understood why they had not got rid of him. They were afraid. They did not know how much he had told the police—

whether he had given them just enough information to stumble on their nudist spoor as he had. And they didn't feel completely safe with merely third-degreeing Big Dan because the beanery owner himself didn't know exactly what Bookie had told the police. It was a three-cornered mixup.

A LITTLE more confidently Bookie Barnes asked. "Was I in trouble with the cops? Is that what it was?"

"Oh, for God's sake!" Dimple-chin was irritated. "Forget it, Barnes. Go grab a drink there."

This, at least, was something that Bookie welcomed. He went to a small table indicated by the hijacker. There, by the bottles, lay a Smith & Weston automatic.

Bookie curbed his instinct to lunge for the weapon. It had to be another gag that the hoods had thought up by their little selves. They were making a test of his amnesia claim for, as sure as that mole on Lora Rawling's hip, Bookie knew there were no bullets in the rod. Leaning over, he could see Dimple-chin's distorted reflection, in a shiny cocktail shaker, watching him.

Bookie poured the last few drops from a bottle of Scotch into his glass. It wasn't half enough. He picked up a new bottle, broke the label, and poured to the brim. He tasted it, made a face, and examined the label. It looked O.K.

Dimple-chin laughed. "Maybe your memory's gone, Barnes, but your taste ain't. That stuff's cut down fifty per cent but you can still drink it. It won't kill you."

Bookie emptied the glass in one long, grateful gulp, despite its reduced potency. "The label looks like the real thing."

"You can never tell, can you, Barnes? Now suppose you get back to your cage and have a good night's sleep. Maybe you'll get your memory back by the morning."

"Swell. I could use some sleep."

The hijacker stuck fingers between his lips and whistled shrilly. In a little while, one of the hoods showed up.

"Put this nut to bed," ordered Dimple-chin, "then get outside. Les will take over at twelve."

Bookie walked out, trailed by the hood. This outfit was beautifully organized. Guards were appointed to make the rounds of the grounds. It was something to remember.

He reached a closed door from which issued a steady, monotonous stream of oaths. The voice sounded familiar. Bookie reached for the knob. The door was locked. Then a heavy shove sent him into the wall.

"That's not your pen, you cuckoo," snapped the hood.

"Excuse me." Bookie walked down the hall and entered his room. A couple of blankets and a pillow were on the sofa.

"Put it there, cuckoo." He produced a pair of handcuffs from his pocket and indicated a steam pipe next to the sofa. "You'll be locked up for the night so you don't hurt yourself."

Bookie started stalling for time. "I wonder what I was before I lost my memory." Casually, he took a couple of steps to the left.

The gun was held carelessly in the hood's right hand and in the other were the handcuffs. But he turned with Bookie.

"You were a magician, cuckoo. You used to get on things like trailers and make whole loads of tobacco disappear right from under your nose. Come on. Stick out your mitt for these bracelets."

"Is that a fact?" Bookie saw a deck of cards on the table. "Maybe if I tried fooling with these I'd remember."

He picked up the deck. The hood shook with laughter. Bookie tried palming the cards, then threw them up in the air a la Houdini. The cards scattered about the room. He knelt and began picking them up in an erratic fashion.

"What a nut! Forget that, cuckoo. Get up."

Bookie ignored the order. As he retrieved the cards, he was inching, on his knees, toward the hood. Now, he could see the pants cuffs and neatly-shined oxfords in front of him. A little closer.

"Get up, I said!"

Bookie did—quicker than the hood had bargained for. His body straightened off the floor and his whole weight was put in the uppercut that cracked on the hood's jaw and chopped him down with the efficiency of a guillotine.

BOOKIE BARNES stepped back to survey his work. He was quite satisfied. Anyone looking into the room would think that the unconscious hood, lying on the sofa covered by blankets with one arm handcuffed to the steam pipe, was Bookie. Everything would be all right till he started yelling and the chances were he'd stay out of the world for a good while. Even the bandage now circled the hood's head.

He hadn't slept in over thirty hours but Bookie felt like a new man. There was a gun in his hand. He opened the door a couple of inches and was in time to see Lora Rawling disappear down the hall. For a change, she was dressed.

He stepped into the hall and locked the door with a key from a chain he had found on the hood. Quickly, silently, he padded to the door from which had issued the stream of familiar oaths. The key chain worked again and he stepped inside. Latch, a sad, maddened, somewhat frightened Latch, sat on the floor, a wrist coupled to a radiator pipe with handcuffs.

Latch was glad to see him. "It's about time someone did something about this, you big, palpitating slab of beef," he hissed. He went on, delving obscenely into Murdock's, the hijackers, the whole trucking business, and several side-issues.

Quickly, Bookie examined the key chain. If only one of them would fit the bracelets! Yes, there it was. He bent over and snapped them open. "What happened?"

"How should I know? That warehouse I was sent to was a mirage. I got halfway up here and somebody flashed a red lantern and I stopped. The next thing I knew I was chained to this thing." He worked his arms, stretching them luxuriously.

"Didn't you first try to see what that red lantern was about before stopping?"

Latch knew it had been a mistake. Defensively, he said: "Why should I figure anything was wrong? I wasn't carrying no load."

"You weren't?" asked Bookie. "Didn't she seem to drive kind of heavy?"

"Say, she did at that, but I just thought the brakes were dragging. You mean—"

"Come on."

They stepped cautiously into the hallway. Big Dan Carp was somewhere in the house but there was no time to try to do something about that now. The important thing, thought Bookie, was to get out of there. Ever since he had seen that phoney government label on that bottle of Scotch an idea was buzzing in him. The first thing to do was to make sure of it.

They stole down the hallway. Noises, the tinkle of ice in glasses, loud laughter came to them from different portions of the house but the hallway was silent. As they crept by a door, they could hear the voice of one of the hoods.

He was saying: "I still think we ought to get rid of them. The shams don't know where they went."

They got to the end of the hall and reached the stairhead. The first step creaked and they slid down the banister. They heard steps behind them and froze. Then silence again. They breathed deeply of the open air as they slid through the front door. Taking advantage of the landscaping, they worked their way toward the front gate. Not until they were on the other side of it did they break into a rapid dog-trot.

Using key words, trying to save his breath, Bookie explained what had taken place. Soon, he stopped talking as their pace quickened and they began to feel the strain of the unaccustomed form of exercise. They reached the end of the side road and, without pause, swung toward town.

Behind them, they heard the sound of an engine. Each took a side of the road. There was no need for words. The sound drew nearer. It was an old rattletrap, ambling along, the youthful driver paying scant attention to the passing scenery but a good deal more to his girl who snuggled close to him.

As it pulled abreast of them Bookie leaped on the running board by the driver's side and Latch took the other. The girl screamed—a long, beautiful scream.

Bookie grabbed the wheel and with one hand reached over and bodily yanked the driver out of the open car. "What's the idea of the one-arm driving?" he yelled. "It's dangerous! You don't deserve a car!"

Latch finally managed to get the girl out of the car and they were off. He patted an ear, with a handkerchief, where she had bitten him, and said: "It would be nice to know where I was going—just for conversation."

"We're trying to find out why Judson Parrish was killed. Now, shut up."

The Parrish homestead, when they reached it, seemed quiet. Bookie parked some distance away and they approached it on foot. Bookie had his eye on that large building next to the garage. The one the old woman had called Judson Parrish's laboratory. They were stepping into the driveway when it suddenly happened.

What seemed to be a dozen simultaneous jets of flame appeared and merged, spreading with destructive rapidity over the building that was next to the garage.

CHAPTER FIVE
BLAZE OF GLORY

EVEN IN the few seconds that astonishment paralyzed Latch and Bookie Barnes, the flames completely sheathed the building in one yellow, crackling, sparkling mass.

"That's got the earmarks of gasoline or oil if I know my ABC's of arson," pronounced Latch.

In the penumbra of light that was pushing out from the burning edifice, Bookie saw a small, dark figure. "Come on," he yelled.

They gave chase, racing down the driveway, past the hungry heat into the cold darkness of the gardens beyond. The figure could not move quickly and they rapidly overhauled it with Bookie managing to grab at a pair of thin shoulders. It was the old lady—Grandma Parrish.

Bookie felt something moist and slippery on the dress over her shoulders. He ran his fingers down her sleeve and felt her hands. It was oil.

Bookie looked back toward the house from which horrified shouts could now be heard. He pulled his eyes away from that blazing splendor with difficulty. "So you started the fire," he stated.

The old woman had regained her breath by now and did not appear too frightened. "I guess," she said ruefully, "I'm not going to have as much fun now as the last time a man chased me."

"Don't talk in circles," he said roughly. "Did your granddaughter or Henry Daly help you or was this your own idea?"

"Entirely my own."

"Why did you do it tonight?"

"I decided on it after talking with you in the truck. You didn't seem dumb enough and I wanted all evidence destroyed completely lest you stumble on the right answer."

Still some miles away, they could hear the sirens of fire engines. Bookie asked: "He was an engraver, wasn't he?"

"Yes. How did you find out?"

"I saw a sample of his work. A government label on a phoney bottle of Scotch. A good job, too."

"Yes. That was the trouble."

"It's over my head," complained Latch. "Who's this about?"

"Judson Parrish," explained Bookie. "He was an engraver and he made queer labels and things for our friends of the nudist colony. All his plates and anything that might prove it are probably burning up in there at this moment."

"That's right," Mrs. Parrish said complacently.

"Did your grandson also make counterfeit money?" asked Bookie Barnes.

"No. If he had I wouldn't mind telling you, because you could no longer prove it."

"How did it start?"

"Like all those things. At first he used to amuse himself by making all kinds of imitations of stamps and labels and things in his workshop there. Then I suppose he needed a lot of money and this fellow—I don't know his name—got hold of him."

"Has he a dimple on his chin?"

"That's the one. I saw you out of the crematory window, chasing him this afternoon."

"Yes," said Bookie. "He wanted to know what you were going to do with Judson Parrish's body. Go on."

THE OLD lady said: "So my grandson did a job for this dimpled individual and, of course, once was enough. He had to continue acceding to their demands out of sheer blackmail. They'd give him the original design, and he'd cut a plate for it and then they'd roll it off on a printing press they had."

"For what else did your grandson make labels, other than liquor?"

"For playing cards, tobacco, everything like that."

"I think I get the picture," he said. "Dimple-chin and his outfit would steal the stuff, pack it, Judson Parrish would be made to supply the labels and any tax stamps that were needed, and they'd resell it. Modern design in bootlegging."

The fire engine arrived and started running out hose. The fire, however, had already reached its zenith and was expending itself on the collapsing walls.

Bookie Barnes asked: "When did you find all this out?"

"Naturally, we suspected something was wrong for some time but yesterday morning—it seems like a year ago—he confessed the whole thing to us."

"Us who?"

"Carol, Henry Daly, and I. Of course, we were shocked and our first instinct was to go to the police but we couldn't do that without ruining Judson and putting a black mark on the whole family. But Judson was tired and frightened of the whole thing. He found out that the gang was now stealing entire truckloads of goods off the highways and he wanted to get out of it."

"It clicks," said Bookie. "I suppose he found out they were going to lift my load of tobacco."

"Yes. He told us that he would go down where it was supposed to happen—some place on the Boston Post Road near Norwalk—and that he'd make them let him be quit of it or threaten to tell the police. We begged him not to do it but he insisted. Carol and Henry went after him and I guess you know the rest."

"They refused to be scared," Bookie Barnes completed, "and when he started to threaten too much they killed him and dropped the body in Latch's trailer. But why did those two steal his body?"

"What would you do?" snapped the old woman. "He was dead and the least we could try to do was save his and the family's name. The futile satisfaction of finding which of a dozen thugs shot him wouldn't bring him back to life again and would certainly drag him through the slime of the newspapers. That's why, at my age, I've become a pyromaniac."

The fire hose was working at last but there was little left to save. Silhouetted in the spending fire, Bookie could see the shapely figure of Carol Parrish. "She's all right," he remarked. "Plenty of nerve—and good eyes."

"Carol's marrying Henry Daly," the old lady said defensively.

"Let him. I wouldn't want a show window like that for my wife. I'd have to spend the rest of my life hitting men who whistled after her. I'd rather do the whistling myself."

"You got what you want here, Bookie," said Latch. "What about those gorillas?"

Bookie looked at his watch. It was a few minutes after twelve and he realized that the hood who lay unconscious in his place was supposed to be relieved of guard duty at midnight.

"That damned tobacco!" he yelled. "We've got to get it before they powder on us."

THEY WERE back in the rattletrap car now and, desperately, Bookie tugged at the choke and jammed his heel against the starter button, trying to get the balky motor going. Someone was running toward them.

"Do we like him?" asked Latch.

The running figure was the sheriff. Bookie said, "No."

The sheriff reached them and Latch's foot kicked out to trip him even as the rattletrap gave a hopeful sputter and unexpectedly started. Bookie turned the crate around and, as they got under way, there was a wild shot from the sheriff that caught one of the tires.

Dangerously, the rattletrap swerved and it was hardly more than the strength of their wishes that kept it upright.

Bookie's foot pressed down to the floorboard. The shattered tire peeled off and they rode on the rim.

A few minutes later, Bookie Barnes stopped the car near Camp Verde. "We've got to get those trucks out," he said, "before they find their gorilla missing."

They passed through the gate and were stealing down the driveway before they saw that something was wrong. Lights were blinking on and off in the house and shadowy figures were combing the grounds with searchlights. The alarm had already been given! Nearby, there was a shout. "Here they are!"

Someone sprang at Bookie. Instinctively, he ducked and he could feel the breeze of a heavy club as it whizzed by his head. His fists shot out. The right missed, the left connected and his way was no longer barred.

Dark shapes, preceded by shafts from flashlights were bearing down on them.

Reminded of his gun, Bookie pulled it out and pushed down the safety. "Over there!" he yelled at the top of his lungs. "By the fence!"

Like a well-drilled platoon of fireflies, the flashlights swerved to the right. Bookie and Latch raced for the house. Their best chance was to get inside it and hide while the grounds were being curry-combed for them.

They reached the front door and at last they were inside. They heard a gasp and saw one of the hoods at the head of the stairs. He had a sawed-off shotgun.

The weapon looked efficient and Bookie didn't hesitate. He pressed the trigger of his gun once, and then once again, before the mobster fell.

Almost at the same instant, there was a scream. That would be Lora Rawling. Now the house was alive with yells and running feet. They reached the stairhead and blindly pushed into the first room they met and slammed shut the door. Then, they saw someone peering out the window.

It was Big Dan Carp.

THE BEANERY owner's face beamed delightedly. "Why, you sonuvaguns! I was sure worried for you guys."

Bookie raised his gun to a business level. "Good for you, Dan. You can worry as long as you want—provided you don't try to shout any warning."

Big Dan's head twisted questioningly.

"Are you crazy?" demanded Latch.

"By no means. I knew Dan was the ringleader of this bunch when he jumped the sheriff this afternoon. He was afraid the sheriff wouldn't let us go and that I'd tell him what that other truck crossing his bridge meant. That cop had a gun in his mitt and diving for it was a pretty brave act. That's what set me thinking straight. If he was brave enough to jump a gat now, why didn't he have the guts to stand up with us in his hash-house against those three guys?"

They could hear footsteps running down the hall and then a yell as the hood's body was found. Big Dan eyed Latch and Bookie warily and didn't speak. Bookie answered for him.

"He didn't get in on that fight because he had to be outside supervising the switching of the trailers while the muggs kept us busy fighting. When the switch was completed, he appeared with the axe and that was the signal to his torpedoes to powder. He came up with me here because he didn't know how much I suspected and he was worried. He wanted to be sure I'd be trapped here and even after I was, he kept up the fake by putting a bandage around his head to make me think he'd gotten the same medicine from Lora Rawling."

"That doublecrosser!" Latch was building up to a good mad.

"Stay clear of him," cautioned Bookie, "so I can pot him if he wants to play."

Big Dan finally spoke. "You're way off, Bookie. That's pretty thin figuring."

"The hell it is! Only you would know the timing and the comings and goings of the trucks and their schedules and you always heard the drivers talking of their loads. You knew what to hijack. Only you could have known I'd be meeting Latch at your place. You probably kept a moron like Pete behind your counter because a guy like that wouldn't realize that something funny was going on."

Latch said something but Bookie Barnes didn't hear him. A connecting door had slid open and Dimple-chin stood there, gun in hand. Both Big Dan and Latch were turned away from him. His gun was trained on Latch's back and Bookie knew that if he tried to shift to get a straight bead at the gangster, a halfdozen bullets would be sent into his friend's back.

Bookie hoped that he had given no sign of noticing Dimple-chin. He said: "Dan, you were very smart to wash your hands of this outfit. I've called the cops like you told me and after we've got this bunch pickled away, you and I will work this racket strictly for ourselves."

Latch said, "Huh?"

Big Dan's face was a picture of puzzlement. Bookie saw Dimple-chin's wrist move. Baffled fury and vengeance were written over him as he emptied his gun at Big Dan Carp.

At the same instant, Bookie dived, football fashion. He collided with the gangster and they went down in a snarling tangle. Latch's heel came down and Dimple-chin stopped struggling.

There was no time to think. They realized it would be only a matter of seconds before the whole gang was down on their necks. Bookie picked up Dimple-chin and draped him over his shoulder like a sack of sugar. He didn't have to look to know that Big Dan Carp was coffin-filler.

LATCH AND Bookie, with his burden, ran out and down the hall. Shouts and yells were all around them and no longer served to place their hunters. A screaming virago swooped on them. Besides a good shape, Lora Rawling had good lungs. Bookie backhanded her with his free arm and felt the long, clawing groove that she was able to plant across his face.

They reached the rear stairway and half-fell, half-ran down the steps. Bookie shifted Dimple-chin to his other shoulder. Another door and they were in the open.

They could make out three separate buildings in the bright moonlight. They chose the biggest one, the one most likely to be housing the semi-trailers, and ran for it. The noises were farther away now and no one barred their way. They reached their objective to find a capable padlock over the large double doors.

Bookie lifted his gun and a bullet shattered the lock. They went inside. There, at last, were their babies—the two stolen trucks. Bookie tossed Dimple-chin into the cab of number 7.

"Get in," he barked at Latch.

"How about the other one?"

"I'll fix that."

Bookie threw open the hood of tractor number 16. He reached inside, grabbed a bunch of wires and yanked. That would hold it there. It would take hours to repair the ignition system.

Behind them, the doors swung shut and someone yelled: "They're in here! They're cornered!"

Almost immediately, a Tommy-gun began engraving a semicircle of holes in the doors. Bookie swung into the tractor's cab as the shatterproof windshield shattered. The starter went down and the motor turned over. Bookie was relieved. The bullets had not touched any vital part of the engine—not yet.

Latch bent low over Dimple-chin's inert form.

"Get going," he shouted.

Bookie let up in second. The semi-trailer moved ahead and parted the huge doors like matchwood. Guns were exploding on all sides, as if in a no-man's land, and they hunched low.

A sedan appeared from nowhere and stopped directly in front of them, blocking their path.

Bookie stepped on the gas. The tractor plowed ahead like a heavy tank and smashed aside the barrier with hardly more than a sound of irritation. Down the driveway, through the gates—they were on the road again.

In a little while they would be back with the police. If not the whole gang then most of it would be picked up— but the trucks and the tobacco were safe.

Bookie and Latch sighed their relief. Dimple-chin— their peace-offering to the sheriff—didn't move.

It was some minutes before Latch felt sufficiently controlled to speak. "That first guy who was murdered, Bookie. That Judson Parrish. Who fixed him?"

"Dan Carp. He was the head of the gang and Parrish naturally went to him with his threats. They didn't take, and

Carp killed him and later disposed of the body by throwing it in the trailer."

"Then it's lucky this baby shot him because he was headed for the electric chair."

"No, he wasn't. This damned fool Parrish family got rid of the body and any other shred of evidence that might have convicted Dan Carp."

"Say!" Latch looked at Bookie queerly. "Don't tell me you egged this guy here into killing Dan Carp because you knew he'd be able to get away with the murder!"

Bookie Barnes didn't reply. He leaned forward as if trying to urge a little more speed out of the cumbersome semi-trailer.

MURDER WITHOUT DEATH

IT LOOKED LIKE BOOKIE'S LUCKY NIGHT WHEN THE SVENGALI-EYED MAN IN BLACK OFFERED HIM A C-NOTE JUST TO JOCKEY A HEARSE ON A SHORT 60-MILE HAUL. BUT THE LITTLE FUNERAL PROCESSION TURNED INTO A NIGHTMARE WHEN THE BIG TRUCKER DISCOVERED THAT THE BLACK-GARBED STRANGER WHO RODE BESIDE HIM WAS A FUGITIVE FROM THE COFFIN IN BACK.

CHAPTER ONE
STABBING EYES

"**THE DAMNED** Svengali," muttered Bookie Barnes.

Bookie disliked being stared at as much as anyone and the piercing eyes of the man in the black coat, following his every movement, were particularly annoying. They seemed to have a hypnotic, X-ray quality and, as Bookie leaned over to chain up the tailboard of his trailer, he could feel those small, beady orbs drilling into the layers of clothing right through to his appendix.

Bookie did not have the appearance of a sensitive plant. He was big and chesty and looked like the "after" part of one of those before-and-after ads. Bookie might have been thinking something of the same for he told himself that it was silly to let the Svengali get him. In, of all places, the New York terminal of Murdock Motor Freight, Inc.!

The terminal was a bedlam of noise and seeming confusion as the huge semi-trailers were backed up against the platform and loaded for the nightly runs which ranged from Maine to Pennsylvania. It was not the kind of place to promote worry. The air was thick with the fumes of exhausts, the yells and oaths of drivers, the squeals of chains, pulleys, and obstinate crates, the rumble of tractors' motors and heavy-duty tires.

With a grinding clash of fenders, the light
truck was sent swerving crazily to the side.

Deliberately, Bookie Barnes straightened up and
turned to face the Svengali. There he was, standing by the
gas pump, next to the night foreman. Despite the mild
weather, the offending stranger wore gloves and his coat
was buttoned to the neck with the collar turned up. A hat,
also black, was tilted low and what could be seen of the
face was white and fleshless. Bookie stared back, unwav-
eringly, into the black, pinpoint irises, telling himself that
if it weren't for the foreman he'd go over and close those
eyes to his own satisfaction.

It was Bookie Barnes who surrendered and first dropped his eyes. Angrily, feeling he was being a fool, he turned back to the semi-trailer to check the twenty-seven variously colored lights and six reflectors. In a few minutes he'd be shoving the tractor-trailer combination up to Bridgeport, Connecticut.

But he was unable to rid himself of the uncomfortable feeling and called to Latch, another of Murdock's drivers, who was trying not to notice a flat tire on his truck unit.

"That beanbag in the blackout clothing by the pump," said Bookie. "What do you make of him?"

Latch looked and shrugged. "A guard or something."

But Svengali, Bookie knew, could not be one of the guards recently hired by Murdock Motor Freight to keep an eye on the transportation of war orders. They were easy to spot—competent and solid with tomato-red faces. This Svengali staring at him would keel over from a strong whiff of onions.

With a relief that shamed him, Bookie swung up into the cab of the tractor and began to pull away from the platform. Another ten seconds and he'd be in the clean night air, away from those eyes. He heard a shout and saw the foreman flagging him back. He pulled the emergency and dismounted from the cab knowing, without question, that the delay had something to do with the stranger of the piercing eyes.

The foreman came up. "You'll have to drop that, Barnes," he said. "I've got another job for you."

"What's wrong now?"

"Nothing. You're taking a half-ton Chevvy up to Bridge-port."

"Me?" Bookie bridled. He had been with Murdock for three years. The inexperienced drivers were given the odd jobs with the smaller trucks.

"Only this once," said the foreman placatingly. He nodded toward the Svengali. "I wouldn't pick you except that he insists."

"I don't get it. Why does he insist on me?"

"He's been sizing up my boys and he figures that you look the toughest, that you can take care of yourself in a pinch."

So that was why Svengali had been looking him over. "What will I carry in that half-tonner?" asked Bookie suspiciously.

"Oh, nothing heavy. You'll have no trouble at all. It's just a coffin. And what's inside it."

BOOKIE BARNES shook his head decisively. "Not on your tintype. I'm a truck driver—not an undertaker's stooge. Get yourself a couple of Valkyries."

"He wants you to drive it," responded the foreman, "and if you don't want to you can turn in your time card."

Bookie hesitated. He liked his job. "Since when do we go in for this kind of hauling?" he asked.

"We're in business and when we're offered five hundred bucks to drive from here to Bridgeport that's a profit. Besides, he says he'll give you a hundred dollar bonus. He says."

That, decided Bookie, made a difference. With Svengali dishing out a century for driving a coffin up to Bridgeport it would be worth it—especially when the alternative was losing his job. Bookie nodded. "It's a deal."

"I thought you'd see it the hundred-dollar way. Get going, Barnes. The box is loaded outside. I'll send him out to you."

"You mean that Svengali's coming along?"

"Stop arguing." The foreman was becoming irritated. "There's a law about someone having to travel along with a coffin and if there isn't he's paying for the privilege."

"How about Latch or Steve Czerno?" asked Bookie with an uneasiness he couldn't explain. "They'd be glad to drive the coffin for a hundred buck tip."

"I told you the guy wants you! If—" The foreman suddenly grinned. "Say, I'll bet you're scared."

"Grow up," muttered Bookie. Without further word, he strode out and found the small truck by the curb. He looked inside and saw the plain, oblong box. A tag attached to one end gave the occupant's name, *Marcus Lunding,* and an address on a street off the Boston Post Road in Bridgeport.

He went around to the front, got into the driver's seat, and turned over the motor. A few moments later, the Svengali came out and sat next to Bookie, saying: "How do you do."

Bookie didn't reply. A Murdock driver named Lou Selinski rumbled by and gave two mocking blows on the horn when he saw Bookie in the small truck. Viciously, Bookie jammed into gear and the vehicle jerked forward. He decided that the trip to Bridgeport would be made in record time.

They raced through upper Manhattan and the Bronx as silent as the coffin-enclosed corpse of Marcus Lunding in the back. Occasionally, as they passed street lamps, Bookie would glance at his companion. The Svengali looked straight ahead. Without being able to see the eyes, the face was expressionless and the flesh, on closer inspection, seemed more yellow than white.

They had reached the Boston Post Road when Bookie heard a slight rustle and saw a gloved hand extending something. He could make it out by the dashboard light. A hundred dollar bill.

"That's for you." The Svengali's voice was soft and he still didn't bother to turn his head.

Bookie pocketed the bill. "That's a lot of money to give away for a trip like this," he said.

"It is. I hope you will spend it wisely and not on gambling or liquor. Please stop at the next gas station as I would like to make a phone call."

Bookie did so. He watched the Svengali as he went with slow, measured steps into the station. His feelings had been baseless and unreasonable, Bookie told himself. The Svengali sounded like a reformer—a harmless crackpot whose hobby was staring at people.

Svengali completed his call and they moved ahead. Bookie was feeling a little friendlier but there was still something he couldn't understand. He said: "Why did you ask to get a driver who could take care of himself in a pinch?"

"For good reason, but I hope you won't have to find out."

Bookie frowned. "Has it something to do with Marcus Lunding—the body we're carrying?" he asked bluntly.

"A great deal."

"Was this Marcus Lunding a friend of yours?"

"Yes."

Bookie felt he was getting no place rapidly. "What did he die from?" he fished.

"He didn't just die," was the reply. "He was murdered."

BOOKIE BARNES' foot pushed down for more speed. He looked at his companion. The Svengali still did not face him but continued gazing ahead, down the dark road.

"He was murdered," the soft voice repeated, "and he shall be avenged."

"I don't get it."

"Wouldn't you go after the murderer of someone dear to you?"

"Sure, but didn't the police get the killer?"

"No. That will be my job. The police don't even know of the murder of Marcus Lunding."

It wasn't making sense. Bookie lit a cigarette to be able to examine his companion by the light of the match. The patch of face between upturned collar and hat seemed to be set in cement. The Svengali was not jesting.

Bookie asked: "Do you know who killed Marcus Lunding?"

"Yes. Three are responsible. Three rotten members that comprised his family—"

"I'm beginning to think you're a crackpot," said Bookie Barnes with a bluntness that surprised himself. "You ought to be lassoed before you start making trouble."

Though he was watching the road as they passed by Larchmont, Bookie could feel the unoffended shrug.

"I don't blame you for thinking so," was the reply, "but I'm saner than I ever was. Marcus Lunding's murder opened my eyes to a lot of things."

"I still can't understand why the police don't know about the murder," said Bookie.

"They simply weren't informed."

"Where did it happen?"

"In New Jersey. The Palisades."

"There are cops even in Jersey."

"They didn't witness the murder and no one told them it had taken place."

Bookie wondered if he should stop at the next police station and have his passenger measured for a padded cell. But maybe there was something to it. Bookie decided to wait a while and let him talk. He asked: "How was the guy murdered?"

"Marcus Lunding went for his customary walk to watch the sunset. He had a summer home on the Palisades. The murderers stole up behind him and pushed him off a cliff. It was just a twenty-five or thirty foot drop—just enough to break his neck."

"What do you mean by the murderers?" asked Bookie. "Just one killer was enough to shove him off the cliff."

"It makes little difference which of the three did it. They were all part of the scheme."

"Did you actually see the murderer?"

"No, but I know who was responsible."

Bookie Barnes flicked his lights in recognition to a passing truck and sighed. "I don't get the picture. If you didn't make all this up out of reclaimed rubber then you have a reason for telling it to me. I want to know that reason."

"I see I chose my driver well," the Svengali said. "I wanted one with both muscles and intelligence."

Bookie's fingers whitened as they tightened on the steering wheel in an effort to control the pointless anger rising in him. "Stop talking in circles," he snapped.

"I'll try," was the mild response. "What do you want to know?"

"You didn't give me a hundred bucks just to drive this scooter sixty miles. And how come you paid all that dough to Murdock on a short-haul for a coffin?"

"I'm wealthy. Money means little to me."

"If you're wealthy that's because you don't throw your dough away for no reason. Besides, it's nine o'clock in the evening and it's the wrong time to pick for taking Marcus Lunding's body back to his family and—"

"The time is well calculated and perfect," interrupted the smooth voice.

"—and the custom is to send coffins by hearse on short distances and by train on longer runs." Bookie's voice became harsher as he warmed to his argument. "There's something phoney going on and a hundred bucks doesn't make me like it. How could you get a burial certificate on Lunding without the cops knowing? A thing like a broken neck is reported automatically. And—"

"And what?"

"What's your angle? You say you were Marcus Lunding's friend but that means nothing."

IF THE Svengali intended replying, Bookie never heard it. They were passing over a dark stretch of the Post Road and, automatically, Bookie glanced at his rear view mirror as a beam of light crossed it. A car had just pulled out of a side intersection and was bearing down on them at a fast clip.

The approaching car was heavy—in those split seconds, it looked like a sedan to Bookie's experienced eyes—and it gained speed rapidly. Bookie pulled to the safety of the outside lane but the sedan had different ideas. As it came abreast, it swerved to the right, there was the grind of clashing fenders, and the light, half-ton truck was sent swerving crazily toward the side.

Even without the time to think, Bookie knew he couldn't pull the truck out of its stampeding skid. The sedan was already clear, disappearing down the road. Without hesitation, Bookie yanked the wheel to the right, doing perhaps the only thing to avoid crashing over immediately.

With the added, centrifugal momentum, supplied by the wheel turning in the direction of the skid, the light truck went into a spin. Six or seven times the car spun around in widening circles, each time slower, till finally it jumped the shoulder by the edge of the road and settled on its side in a shallow ditch.

For a full minute, Bookie Barnes lay stunned in a state of semi-consciousness. As he came to, he breathed deeply and moved his limbs. Nothing seemed broken. Fortunately, the car had slowed down considerably before turning over into the ditch. Then Bookie realized that his companion was missing.

He climbed out of the side-turned truck. The Svengali, who had either jumped or been thrown clear in the crash, was struggling to his feet. Bookie noticed that the coffin had also been knocked out of the truck and its lid broken off. He looked inside for the corpse of Marcus Lunding. It was empty.

Bookie went toward the Svengali who was silhouetted by the light of the headlamps which had somehow stayed on. The bottom half of his coat was ripped but he seemed to have suffered little other damage. As Bookie neared him, he noticed a small object on the ground and picked it up. It was the Svengali's wallet which had dropped from the torn clothing. He opened it. The identification card read: *Marcus Lunding.*

CHAPTER TWO
SHARP NAILS

"**SO MARCUS LUNDING** was murdered!" said Bookie Barnes with all the sarcasm he could inject into his voice.

The other still breathed deeply but managed to reply: "Yes, he was."

"You liar!" yelled Bookie. "There's no corpse in that coffin. This is your wallet. You're Marcus Lunding and you're going to tell me what it's all about!"

The other didn't reply.

The accident to his truck—which Bookie knew had been no accident—the lies he had listened to, the corpse which didn't exist, all caused a welling fury in him. He reached out with one big paw, grabbed the black coat and yanked Lunding forward. The buttons tore and the coat parted—to reveal that Marcus Lunding's neck was set in a steel brace.

"Do you understand now?" asked the soft voice. "Those three did murder me, they did break Marcus Lunding's neck."

Bookie released his hold. "I'm sorry. I couldn't guess what it was about."

The soft voice became bitter. "If medical science was able to perform miraculous patchwork and I still breathe, that does not make the crime lesser. I'm as good as murdered. Worse! I'm useless. I'm hardly past forty but I look all of sixty."

It was true. "Then what's the idea of the vaudeville act with the coffin?" demanded Bookie.

"It's no act. I want Amos and Susan and Frank to see where they have put me. I want them to pay for their crime."

"Why didn't you tell the cops about getting shoved off a cliff?"

"That would make it too easy—for those three."

Bookie moved away. He returned the empty coffin to the back of the truck, then took stock of the damage. The side on which the car rested had not caved in and the motor seemed all right. However, a tire was blown and the wheels were probably out of line.

Bookie lit a cigarette and waited. Marcus Lunding would hold, he thought. There was nothing to do now. Even if he wished to, there was nothing he could tell the police. It was no crime to hire a truck to carry an empty coffin.

They were near Greenwich and those few automobiles that stopped to offer assistance were waved on by Bookie. It was not long before his ears, sensitive to the throb of motors, picked up the sound for which he was waiting. It was, Bookie knew, one of Murdock's semi-trailers rumbling toward them. He stepped out into the road and blinked a flashlight in his hand, bringing the tractor-trailer unit to a halt.

It was Lou Selinski who looked out at Bookie from the cab of the tractor. He took in the situation and began to roar. A safety driver—one with a silver button in his cap to prove it—had finally met disaster by somersaulting a half-ton truck! Lou Selinski thought it was riotous. Slowly, Selinski grew aware of the cloud over Bookie's face and decided to stop laughing.

The two drivers hauled rope out of the semi-trailer's tool chest. One end was looped over the top edge of the side-turned truck and the other was knotted to the tractor's axle. Barely seeming to strain itself, the tractor pulled forward and toppled the truck right side up.

The drivers removed the rope and Bookie said: "I'll do the rest. Thanks."

"Do you want me to put in a report for you?"

"No." Far from it, in fact. Turning this truck over meant, to Bookie, the loss of his safety record and the bonuses that went with it. He knew not how but he intended to prove that it was not the result of his own negligence.

Lou Selinski nodded and left.

Bookie forced fenders back into position, switched the spare for the blown tire, and then tried the motor. A few sputters and it worked. He beckoned to Marcus Lunding, who had silently watched the proceedings from the background, and they resumed their journey toward Bridgeport—much more slowly this time for one of the front wheels shimmied violently.

In all, barely more than a half-hour had elapsed since the sedan had appeared from the side road, trying to kill Marcus Lunding and Bookie Barnes.

BOOKIE, WHO never carried a gun on his routine hauls voiced aloud his wish to have one now.

"I have a revolver," said Marcus Lunding. His coat collar again concealed the brace around his neck and he sat sideways so as to be able to face Bookie.

"I'm beginning to see why you wanted a tough driver. You foresaw something like this."

"I did," Lunding admitted, "only they struck sooner than I had expected."

Bookie guided the wounded truck through Stamford traffic and headed for Darien. He said: "I'd like to know why you expected that crackup. I'd like to know how those three relatives of yours knew you'd be in this truck and where you'd be passing."

"It was that phone call I made before. I telephoned them to let them know I was coming. I even described this truck."

"What did you do that for?"

"I want them to sweat and suffer before they pay for their crime of killing me. I want them to know I'm coming after them."

Bookie Barnes kept his eyes on the dark road and tried increasing his speed by a couple of miles. The sooner the coffin was delivered and his job finished, the better he would feel.

"Do you still think I'm crazy?" asked Marcus Lunding.

"I've met saner guys directing the battle of Waterloo. Why do they want to kill you?"

"My money. I told you I was wealthy and they expect to inherit it. I own a lot of property, bonds, stock, and have nearly a quarter million in cash. But it's not going to them."

"Who gets it?"

"Some of it goes for a church to be erected on a piece of property I own on the Post Road. The rest will be left to create a Marcus Lunding Foundation to combat evil and sin."

And anyone having a little fun, thought Bookie. He asked: "If your playful friends are cut out of your will, what do they gain by trying to kill you?"

"They didn't know they were cut off till I told them so before, over the phone. I told them that I left my money to—" Suddenly, Lunding began to laugh. It was soft, restrained laughter that issued from Marcus Lunding's mouth without causing even the lips to tremble. It was laughter that had no connection with pleasure.

For a long while they drove in silence, Bookie Barnes brooding and wondering how he might save his record as a safety driver and Marcus Lunding lost in his welter of vengeance against the people who had murdered him.

Finally, as they were passing through Fairfield and nearing Bridgeport, Bookie said: "I'd like to get a line on the driver of that sedan that cracked us up."

"That's unimportant," replied Marcus Lunding.

"Maybe it is to you, since you're supposed to be so wealthy, but I've ruined my record. Unless I can get the guy and prove he did it on purpose I lose my bonuses for the next two years. I want to find that sedan."

"You'll probably find it at my home and its driver was probably Amos."

"Where is he?"

"We all live together. Amos is my brother-in-law. His full name is Amos Cook and he's stayed with me since my sister died, hoping to get my money."

"Who are the rest?"

"Frank Cook, my nephew, and Susan Cook, my niece. There are too many of them but that will be remedied."

"What do they do?"

"Amos is an architect. There's a sample."

They had reached the outskirts of Bridgeport and Lunding pointed to a tall building situated on the Post Road. It was intended as a miniature Radio City, the ground floor occupied by a night club and motion picture theatre with offices above.

"Amos planned that," Marcus Lunding continued. "I own all that land next to it and I've willed it for a church."

"What about the other two?"

"There's Amos's son, Frank Cook, a wastrel, and Amos's daughter, Susan Cook. She speaks with honeyed words but covets my money as much as the others. That next block, please."

Bookie turned to the left and, following Lunding's directions, wound down side streets till he was told to stop. They were in front of a large, three-story house. Its lines were severe and solid with no ornamentation. Bookie wondered if that too was an example of Amos Cook's architecture.

Marcus Lunding put something on the seat and stepped out of the truck. "Here's an additional hundred dollars for you," he said. "You will carry the coffin up to the porch and ring the front doorbell. When it's opened, you will set the coffin down in the living-room which will be on your left. Then your job will be done."

"Wait a second," said Bookie. "Won't you come in with me?"

"I'll be around—as long as those three are alive. And in case you don't intend to follow my instructions, remember that I carry a revolver."

Marcus Lunding walked away. Bookie called to him and leaned out. The street was dark, and quiet, and empty. Lunding had probably disappeared into a grove of trees adjoining the house where the Cooks lived. Bookie shrugged. He took the hundred dollar bill on the seat, went around to the back of the truck, opened the doors, and hoisted the light coffin to his shoulders.

WITH ONE hand, Bookie Barnes steadied the coffin over his back and pushed the doorbell with the other. It was a full minute before he heard movement from inside the house.

As the door finally opened and Bookie stepped over the threshold into the lit hallway, there was a scream and a fist hit him on the chin. The blow was light and he whirled to find that his attacker was a young girl.

Normally, she was pretty. But at the moment, she wore a faded wrapper, her face was twisted with rage, and the long, reddish hair dropped over head and shoulders in twisted tangles. She descended on Bookie furiously, kicking and pummeling him with her small fists. Protecting himself as best he could, he dropped the coffin and stumbled over it, falling to the floor.

She leaped after him and the pointed shoes kicked as she screamed: "Leave us alone! It won't work! Do you understand that? We're not scared!"

Bookie felt a long slit of blood, probably from a fingernail, and decided to stop being chivalrous with the redheaded vixen. The next time one of the pointed shoes came within range he grabbed and twisted. She fell in a heap and he pinioned her shoulders against the coffin.

"Now cut it out," he snapped. "I stopped having fun after the first pint of blood."

"We're not scared!" She struggled to get at him and the words came out explosively, as if from a broken exhaust. "We're not. Go back and tell that to your boss."

He kept her away, thankful for his longer reach. "We've got our wires crossed. My boss wouldn't know you from a Panzer division."

"You get out of here and go back to the Twittering Bird and tell him!"

"The Twittering Bird?" Then Bookie remembered. It was the name of the night club occupying the ground floor of the building Marcus Lunding had pointed out—the one planned by Amos Cook. "You're still off your course, girlie."

"Don't tell—" For the first time she seemed to notice his windbreaker and peaked cap. "Oh. I'm sorry. I thought you were one of Colombo's gunmen but you don't look like that."

"If this is a sample of how you greet Colombo's gunmen I'm glad I'm not one of them."

He thought it safe to take his hands away from her shoulders. She pulled together her wrapper and brushed back her hair and a tinge, as red as the hair, spread over her face. They stood up.

"It was a mistake," she said. "When you walked in with that coffin I thought it was another one of their attempts to intimidate us. They've been sending us threatening notes and obituary notices and it seemed—" She caught her breath. "If you're not one of Colombo's men what is this coffin?"

He pointed to the tag and she bent over and read the name. Her body stiffened perceptibly but there was no outcry. At least one thing was correct, Bookie thought. There was little love between Marcus Lunding and his niece.

He said: "It's empty. I'm just delivering it for your uncle. Marcus Lunding is your uncle, isn't he?"

Susan Cook nodded. "This must be more of his browbeating."

"He sent it because you're supposed to have helped shove him off a cliff and murder him—after a fashion."

"I don't understand." Susan Cook considered the coffin speculatively, with no fright.

The phone rang and Bookie followed her into a bleak living-room. Without much hope, he looked around for a whiskey bottle, then sat down and listened as she spoke into the phone.

"He hasn't shown up yet, Mr. Jason, but he must be around... He sent a sample of his macabre humor by some truck driver... A coffin with his name on it... I'll tell him, Mr. Jason." She replaced the receiver.

Bookie asked: "Who's this Jason looking for your uncle?"

"Henry Jason. He owns the building where the Twittering Bird is. If you don't mind, I'm expecting a visitor."

Bookie didn't move. "I'm looking for a sedan with smashed fenders on the right hand, side."

"My father owns a sedan but I don't know about the fenders. I'm afraid you'll have to leave now."

"Take it easy," said Bookie. "You're more than a match for me but I'm sticking around till I find that sedan. It turned over my truck and it'll cost me bonuses or even my job if I can't prove it wasn't my fault."

"I see. You're just another victim of my dear uncle."

"I don't get it."

"It's simple. After my mother died, Marcus Lunding made it a hell for us. He's taken advantage of our dependence on him and he thinks we want to kill him. It's gotten to the point where I'd grab the first man who'd flash a wedding license."

AND GOD help that man, thought Bookie. "It has nothing to do with me, Miss Cook, but Marcus Lunding seems to think that your father and brother and you are responsible for breaking his neck. He's hanging around some place with a gun. You ought to tell the police."

"He's only trying to scare us. I haven't heard about any broken neck and he's probably lying. Have you a cigarette?"

He gave her one. "Did your uncle phone here a couple of hours ago?"

"Thanks. We're not even allowed to smoke in the house though he does. There was a phone call that might have been from him. My father took it and left right after."

In time to intercept the truck, thought Bookie. "And where's your brother, Frank?"

"Probably chasing Margit," Susan Cook said with a venom that made him wonder.

"If you're not after Marcus Lunding's dough why don't the three of you move out?" asked Bookie. "Your father's an architect. He makes dough. He made that building for Jason on the Post Road."

"That was the first job he had in a long time and Henry Jason hasn't even paid him for it." There was the sound of a car in the driveway. "That must be father now," she said.

"Why wasn't your father paid for it?"

"He and Mr. Jason had some sort of fight and he quit before the job was completed."

They heard the front door open and a moment later Amos Cook entered. His hair was of a darker red than his daughter's and, when he spoke, his voice had a rasping, belligerent quality. "Is that coffin more of Colombo's dirty—" He stopped as he saw Bookie.

"That's one of Uncle's tricks," Susan Cook explained. "This man delivered it."

Amos Cook barked: "Get out of my house, Barnes."

"So Marcus Lunding told you my name when he phoned. He also told you enough to send you chasing after my truck."

Amos Cook advanced then stopped when he realized Bookie's impressive size. "My brother-in-law told me enough to know you're a crook. Don't think you'll get away with it because we'll contest the will every inch of the way!"

Bookie frowned. It sounded like double talk but he remembered Marcus Lunding's queer laughter when reminded of his will. He asked: "What has Lunding's will got to do with me?"

"You know very well," Amos Cook shouted. "We've suffered here for years and now he's leaving his money to you. But we'll break that will on insanity grounds!"

There was the answer to Marcus Lunding's laughter. He had phoned his brother and informed him he was changing his will in favor of a truck driver—a stranger! It was delicate torture—the most effective for the Cook family.

Bookie said: "I doubt if that goon left me the steel brace around his neck but you're a little premature. He thinks himself as good as murdered but you'll have to finish the job before you start contesting his will."

"Do you accuse me of breaking his neck?"

"No, but he does." What had Marcus Lunding wanted? A driver who could take care of himself? He would start right now, Bookie decided, to do just that.

Without further word, Bookie stood up and walked out. He wanted to know if the right hand fenders of Amos Cook's car were damaged. He went down the stoop and around to the driveway where he could make out a sedan. Behind him, Amos Cook had followed him out.

Bookie walked around the sedan, feeling the fenders. They were all smooth. But it proved nothing. Amos Cook, or his son, Frank, might have used some other car. There was the crunching of feet on gravel and Bookie froze.

He looked about but in the half-moon light he could see little. The sound had not come from the direction of the house, where Amos Cook was probably skulking, but from the other side, behind some trees.

Almost as if he had expected it, Bookie heard the explosion of a gun from the other side of the car and immediately a sharp gasp. Then again silence.

He moved over a few feet and kicked something. He picked it up. It was a revolver. He reached inside the car and threw on the headlamps. Not far away he could see a form on the ground. As Marcus Lunding had promised, there was one less Cook.

Amos lay dead in the dirt.

CHAPTER THREE
LYING TONGUES

"**P**ATIENCE IS the hallmark of an intelligent man."

This item of bombast was addressed to Bookie Barnes and issued from the lips of a motorcycle cop named Felton—the first to arrive at the scene. Susan Cook was also present, huddled in the corner of a sofa, apparently more shocked than grieved by the sudden death of her father.

"I tell you Marcus Lunding is running around loose," snapped Bookie. "You'd better get him before he kills any more Cooks."

"So he's loose," soothed Felton, "and I can only be in one place. The boys will be along in a little while and he'll be attended to. I'd still like to know how you let your prints get on this gun, Bookie."

"I didn't know what it was when I picked it up," Bookie repeated for the tenth time.

"That's not being a smart truck driver. Aside from this guy with the broken neck, who else might have done it?"

"I don't know but someone called Colombo from the Twittering Bird seems to have been pressuring this house. She can tell you about it."

The cop turned to Susan Cook and she said: "He means Luigi Colombo who owns that night club in the Henry Jason building but I don't think he had anything to do with it."

"What has this Colombo against you?"

"It's my uncle. He owns that big piece of land next to the Twittering Bird and he's against night clubs and bars."

"What about it?" prompted Felton.

"My uncle's ruining their business, Colombo claims. He's put up a sort of mission right next door with a lot of psalm-singing and free handouts to anyone that wants it."

The cop nodded. "I've seen it."

"Naturally, the patrons of the club don't like it and it's hurt business. It's the kind of thing that Colombo couldn't prevent legally so he's been sending his gunmen around in an attempt to frighten uncle."

"Uh-huh." Felton rubbed his chin. "You say you don't think Luigi Colombo killed your father. Who did, in your opinion—your uncle?"

"No. My uncle has too much fun tormenting us to want us dead."

"Then who did?"

Susan Cook pointed to Bookie. "Him."

Bookie said: "You mean he."

"The grammar of it will be discussed in due time," announced Felton. "Now, Miss Cook, I've known Barnes for some years and I doubt if you know what you're talking about."

"Is that so?" She straightened up. "I suppose you believe that story of the gun being dropped near his feet and that he just happened to pick it up."

"Why not?"

"It's a very convenient explanation. Then what about my uncle, Marcus Lunding, leaving him all his money?"

She seemed ready to go into action again and Bookie backed away. He said, in answer to Felton's questioning brows: "Lunding's a crackpot. He only phoned in that yarn to Amos Cook to annoy this outfit. Lunding told me he's leaving his dough for a church next to the Henry Jason building."

"Besides," Felton added, "being beneficiary would give you cause to kill Marcus Lunding, not Amos Cook. Lunding isn't dead."

"Not yet," said Susan Cook significantly. "My father threatened to fight that will so this man killed him."

Her voice became shriller as her father's death drove deeper into her consciousness and her hysteria rose. Her voice sounded like police sirens and Bookie was reminded that the Homicide squad would arrive any moment. It would delay him for hours, even longer, he thought glumly, if the Homicide officer gave any credence to her accusations. He had an idea where he might find the sedan that had cracked him up, but a few more hours of delay and it would be a useless hunt.

Bookie cut into the redhead's tirade and said smoothly: "I have to report to my terminal but I'll be back soon."

The cop looked dubious. "I don't think I can allow that, Bookie. Maybe when the department gets here—"

"I'll be back before they arrive. You know me, Felton, and you know where to put your hands on me." Bookie kept talking till he was out and the front door shut behind him.

TWO POLICE cars rounded the corner and came down the block. Bookie Barnes slid behind the wheel of his damaged truck and let out the clutch. He had left the Cook household just in time.

He wasn't too worried about Susan Cook's accusation that he had murdered her father. That could be disproven by Marcus Lunding's will, for Bookie was certain that he was not the beneficiary. Besides, it was an absurdity. He had known these ghouls for only two hours of his life. It was all part of Lunding's scheme, part of his Monte Cristo complex for revenge. That was only the first step in the scheme. The murders of Susan Cook and her brother Frank were yet to follow unless the police corralled Lunding.

Bookie reached his destination and pulled to the curb. He was again on the Boston Post Road, not far from the combination office building and entertainment center Amos Cook had planned for Henry Jason—and for which he had not been paid.

Lots of neon embellished the front of the Twittering Bird and Bookie could see lights from a first floor office window. He could also hear an organ grinding out some psalm. The sound came from Marcus Lunding's mission, a small shack not twenty feet from the Henry Jason building. Lunding had calculated well. It was just the kind of thing to ruin a night club's business—and the projected church right next door would finish the job.

To the right of the Jason building was a parking lot on which were hardly more than two dozen cars. Not very good business for a night club on a Friday night. Deeper in the lot was a lean-to with a few cars parked under its protection. Here, guessed Bookie, were probably the automobiles owned by tenants of the Jason building, by Henry

Jason and Luigi Colombo. These were the cars he wanted to examine.

Bookie left the truck, walked past the Twittering Bird, and turned into the parking lot. There were no attendants. The club's business was probably very bad. He could hear a saxophone wailing in contrast to the muted tones of the mission's organ.

He reached the lean-to and found three cars there. Only one of them was a sedan. He walked around it and felt the front right fender. It was creased. He touched the radiator grille and found it warm. He knew that this was the car that had forced his truck to the side, turning it over.

Bookie considered the sedan, wondering what he should do next. He had heard no sound but gradually grew aware of a bulky figure standing in front of him. The white front of the figure's dinner jacket stood out brightly. It was no doubt a bouncer from the Twittering Bird.

"Having trouble?" asked the bouncer.

"Not unless you start it," replied Bookie whose temper was worn to a razor edge.

The bouncer chuckled confidently. "Feeling sharp, bub?"

"Whose car is this?"

"Can't you cop the tires without knowing whose it is? Live and let live is my motto, bub, but I don't like tire snatchers these days. It ain't patriotic."

"I'm not interested in the tires. I want to know whose car this is."

The bouncer reached out and grabbed Bookie's left wrist. "You better come along and talk to the boss."

"Take your hand off."

"Bub," said the bouncer, "you underwhelm me."

Bookie's right hand moved out and grabbed hold of a lot of face. It was a huge hand and the thumb was under the bouncer's right ear while the small finger reached around in a firm grip under the lobe of the left ear. The hand started to squeeze.

There was an agonized gasp and the bouncer's fingers scrabbled ineffectually to pry the closing vise off his face. Bookie pushed back and jolted the bouncer down on to the sedan's running board. His other hand reached inside the white shirt front and removed a gun. Then Bookie released his hold.

He said, "Tell Luigi Colombo that Bookie Barnes will be around in a little while for explanations," and then walked away.

BOOKIE BARNES entered the lobby of the Henry Jason building and ascended the stairs. That light from the first floor, he was sure, came from Henry Jason's offices—where he was waiting to hear of the return of Marcus Lunding.

Bookie reached the landing, turned left down the corridor, and stopped by a door under which showed a slit of light. He had been right, for the paneling on the door gave Jason's name. He knocked and entered on the response.

Henry Jason turned around in his swivel chair. He was middle-aged and what want ads like to call the executive type. An olive-skinned girl in her twenties sat on the edge of the desk. She was pretty and in a few years she would be plump. At present, the form inside the high-bodiced, Magyar gypsy costume was perfect.

Henry Jason's shrewd eyes took in his visitor. "Are you the truckman Susan Cook mentioned when I phoned her before?" He was no fool.

"Yes. I'm called Bookie Barnes."

"Glad you came up, Barnes. This is Miss Margit Otvos."

"So charmed," exaggerated the girl with a Hungarian accent.

Margit! So this was the girl Susan's brother, Frank Cook, was chasing. At least it showed taste, Bookie thought. He said: "I'd like to see you privately, Jason."

"Speak out, Barnes. I never keep anything from Margit."

"Only your pocketbook," commented the Hungarian.

"There's a sedan downstairs in back of the parking lot," said Bookie. "Do you own it?"

"Is it dark blue with fog lights?" asked Henry Jason.

"That's the one."

"It belongs to Luigi Colombo. I own a roadster."

Bookie frowned. If the night club owner had been behind the wheel of that sedan then it didn't make much sense for Colombo could not have known where the truck would be and when. Marcus Lunding had phoned his home and given that information to his brother-in-law. He wondered if Amos Cook might have borrowed the night club owner's sedan.

"Amos Cook was murdered a half-hour ago," said Bookie.

Henry Jason didn't comment and Margit Otvos said: "How threeling!"

"It doesn't threel me," stated Bookie angrily. "And how about you? What's your angle? What do you want with Frank Cook?"

Henry Jason started to protest but Margit Otvos waved him back. "No, no, let him speak. I like it. You are too gallant, Henry. It becomes boring. Sometimes I even feel you respect me."

"I'm still waiting," said Bookie.

"My name is Margit Otvos and I sing for Luigi. I want little but peace from Frank Cook because he is damp behind his ear and he has no money. Now if Marcus Lunding was interested in me—"

"Margit's morals are unimportant," interrupted Henry Jason hastily. "I'd like to know about Amos's murder."

Finding no reason why he shouldn't, Bookie Barnes outlined the events of the night.

When he was finished, Henry Jason announced with finality: "Amos Cook turned over your truck and later Marcus Lunding, that phoney philanthropist, killed him."

"Maybe," said Bookie, "but some things don't fit. Amos Cook planned this building for you but you didn't pay him. Why?"

"Because he quit the job before it was finished," Jason replied. "We had a fight."

"If you had a fight how come you were friendly enough to phone his home an hour ago?"

"That wasn't a matter of friendship but business. I've been trying to buy two feet of land from Marcus Lunding on the north side of this building. I have to have that extra ground because I want to build a high fence."

"On account of Lunding's mission?" asked Bookie.

"Exactly. I want to shut out the sight of it. Luigi Colombo is my tenant and it's ruining his night club. It's ruining my whole building."

"And you're sure," said Bookie, "that that sedan downstairs doesn't belong to you?"

"I'm sure."

"It's wonderful to be so positive," cooed the Hungarian thrush sardonically.

BOOKIE BARNES entered the Twittering Bird. He managed to get only a faint glimpse of the night club's interior before being whisked away but it was sufficient to reveal the scarcity of patrons and the desperate efforts of the band to inject some gayety into the proceedings.

The whisking away was done by a half-dozen dinner-jacketed bouncers who converged on Bookie. He was eased past a gaping hat-check girl, down the carpeted corridor, and through a door into the office. It was large and comfortable, the windows facing the Boston Post Road, and behind the white mahogany desk sat Luigi Colombo.

The night club owner's fleshy face creased into a pleasant smile. "I expected a big man, Bookie Barnes, and I was right." He indicated the bouncer who had showed fight on the parking lot. "Anyone who can make Freddy do capers has to be big."

Freddy's feet shuffled with embarrassment and the five other bouncers eyed Bookie respectfully.

"And to take his gun, Bookie! Freddy is hurt."

"I didn't feel like being shot in the back as I walked away," said Bookie.

Luigi Colombo chuckled. "My boys are getting soft. In the old days when I was bootlegging whiskey down the Road they could take on twice their number in truck drivers."

The phone jangled and the night club owner reached over and took it. He listened without saying a word, then replaced the receiver.

"What did Henry Jason have to say?" asked Bookie.

Luigi Colombo grinned delightedly to his circle of henchmen. "He guessed it! Should we ask him the ten dollar question?"

"What was it?" persisted Bookie. "Did he warn you to tell me nothing?"

"Don't rush me, Bookie. I'm legitimate now but I still remember how to be tough. Sure that was Henry Jason. He told me that Amos Cook was gunned."

"That's right."

"Too bad it wasn't Marcus Lunding who got it."

"I hear you're having trouble with Lunding."

"Trouble! He doesn't approve of liquor and night clubs and just because he's got an empty lot next door I suffer."

"You'll probably be rid of Lunding. It looks like he killed his brother-in-law."

Luigi Colombo had thick brows and they formed inverted V's as he regarded Bookie with suspicion. "What you meant was that maybe I killed Amos Cook to rig this Lunding for the job. Just forget it, Bookie. Maybe I've been trying to scare Lunding into laying off me but I'm legitimate now and I got my boys here to convince you."

Bookie shrugged. "I'm not interested. There's a dark blue sedan in the back of your parking lot. Do you own it?"

"Yes. Why?"

"That sedan crashed my truck a few hours ago trying to kill Marcus Lunding."

Luigi Colombo yawned. "This time I'm not interested, Bookie. Suppose you go home and take some more nose candy. Give Freddy his gun on the way out."

Bookie decided that the night club owner's counsel was wise. It would be better to get at Luigi some other time— without six bouncers lined up in back. He took the gun from his windbreaker pocket and slid it along the desk.

"Now," said Luigi Colombo as if he were instructing a public school class, "you can grab him and tie him to that chair. Don't make too much noise or you'll wake up the customers."

Bookie's every muscle stiffened, then instantly relaxed. With the gun in Colombo's hand and the half-dozen bouncers on all sides it was senseless to struggle. His teeth clenched and the skin of his face whitened but that was the sole reaction to the rough hands that grabbed at him and shoved him into a chair.

Freddy appeared with a length of clothes-line rope. With the air of an artist, he tied each of Bookie's ankles to a front leg of the chair, knotted his hands in the back, and gagged him securely with a long silk scarf.

His job finished, Freddy spread a hand over Bookie's face. Then he shook his head. "My paws ain't big enough for that trick, bub, but I'll show you—"

"Nothing," completed Luigi Colombo. "First we find out who's using my car to stick me for a bum rap. After that you can make tricks."

The night club owner snapped out the lights and walked out, trailed by his henchmen.

CHAPTER FOUR
RED LIPS

BOOKIE BARNES sat in Luigi Colombo's darkened office, bound to the chair, watching headlamps bear past the windows along the Boston Post Road. From beyond the door, the Twittering Bird's band, hacking away at music, set him on edge.

Freddy was indeed an artist. Bookie's straining and twisting and pressing against the ropes had been unable to make them give a hair. His arms and legs seemed dead and paralyzed and he had stopped trying. The ropes were just tight enough to dam the course of blood to the limbs without stopping it completely.

Bookie's ears picked up the sound of a semi-trailer and he watched its broadside of lights pass by the window. It looked like a job from National Transportation. It was a visible reminder to Bookie that he was getting what he asked for by not minding his own business. When someone like Luigi Colombo smiles pleasantly it's time to forget about bonuses and sedans and get out of—

The door had opened.

The lights came on and Bookie saw Margit Otvos standing there in her abbreviated gypsy costume. How threeling! That's what she would say, thought Bookie bitterly.

Margit did say exactly that and added: "I was hoping we would again meet." She shut the door.

Bookie could make no sound through the gag around his mouth but his eyes followed venomously as she came forward and chucked him under the chin. "How interesting! A helpless man in my power. I would so like to talk with you but you would shout for help if I removed that scarf, would you not?"

Bookie's head shook negatively.

"I hope you will keep your word for your sake," she continued. "I always do. But just in case you don't, do you see this?" She picked up a heavy inkstand from the desk.

Bookie nodded.

"I will drop this right on your head, Bookie dear, the very first time you shout."

He had no doubt but that she would and nodded again. Humming a tune, she undid the scarf.

He wet his lips and swallowed a few times. "Now take off the rope."

"I mustn't do that. Luigi would be furious. I always watch out for my skin and purse. Luigi did put you here, didn't he?"

"Yes."

"Then you will have to stay like that. Where is Luigi?"

Bookie shrugged as well as he could. "I suppose he and Henry Jason are deciding what to do with me. Take off the rope."

"No, my precious. And you mustn't shout because this inkstand is harder than your head. We will have a nice talk and you will tell me all about yourself."

"You haven't finished telling me about yourself," said Bookie. "Finish what you were going to tell me upstairs about Marcus Lunding being interested in you."

"It would be wonderful if he was interested. He has money and he is too old a —— for any other woman to want to take him away. He is not like his nephew. Frank Cook uses vaseline on his hair. I hate men who use vaseline and sing *None But the Lonely Heart,* don't you, my love?"

"I'm not your love," scowled Bookie. "The way I see it, Henry Jason sent you chasing after Marcus Lunding. What did you want from that Svengali?"

"To talk him into selling the two feet of land Henry needs to build that fence. But Marcus Lunding doesn't like liquor and dancing and not even women. Can you imagine somebody not liking me, sugar?"

"Untie this rope."

She laughed and picked up the scarf. "Luigi wouldn't like that. I will have to close your mouth again, my helpless cherub."

Bookie's mind raced. Here was his only chance to get away from that ex-bootlegger and there had to be some way to do it. Slowly, an idea began to filter through his brain. It was a long shot and its chances of working were unlikely as hell but....

He asked: "What time is it?"

"About half past twelve, sugar, but you are not going any place unless Luigi takes you."

He tried the ropes again but could not even feel any sensation in his arms as he twisted them. The long shot was the only chance.

I WANT you to do me a favor," said Bookie Barnes. "I want you to take my cap off my head, open the window, and fling it out into the middle of the Road. It can't get you in wrong with Luigi Colombo because he'll never know about it. After, you can go inside and sing and—"

Margit's laughter broke in. "You take me for a fool, pet."

"Luigi will never know."

"That is not the point. Margit watches out for her own skin and she doesn't do things like that without reason."

Bookie understood. "I can give you money but how do I know you won't doublecross me?"

She was all smiles. "Margit is as honest as the days are long."

"The days are getting shorter now. There's a wallet in my windbreaker pocket. Inside it you'll find two one hundred dollar bills I got from Lunding. You can have them."

Slim, eager fingers probed into his pocket, removing the wallet. "You lied, sugar! There are two hundred four dollars here."

"Those four bucks are mine."

"I will keep them too and in exchange you can watch while I hide them in my garter."

Bookie restrained himself. "All right. Now take off my cap. Hold it by the brim, top side up, and toss it through the window. Try to throw it around twenty feet but be sure it doesn't land on the sidewalk or go past the center line in the road."

With relief, he watched his peaked cap sail out. She shut the window and came back.

"Now I must put back the scarf and leave before Luigi catches me. But first"—she bent over and kissed him full on the lips—"a little gift for my generous pet."

"Wipe off that lipstick," he said ungraciously.

She laughed again and rewound the scarf around the face as securely as it was before. "One can't see the lipstick now, my gallant pet."

The lights snapped off, the door shut behind Margit Otvos, and again he was alone in the dark office—the poorer by $204.

His eyes looked out the window eagerly as he again calculated what chance there was of his cap being noticed. It was after 12:30 now and he had left the New York terminal of Murdock Motor Freight around 8:30. At that time, Latch had had a flat tire on his tractor. Figure fifteen or twenty minutes to change that tire and Latch would be passing the Henry Jason building with the cumbersome semi-trailer shortly after twelve. Too soon.

But Latch would probably make a coffee-and-sinkers stop at some lunch wagon. Irritated by the flat, he was sure to stop by the Waldorf in Westport for his chocolate bar. That would make the timing just right. He'd be due to pass by in a little while.

And when Latch went by he would notice the typical truck driver's cap in the middle of the road. Maybe not the other drivers, but he would. He was one of the wild-cat drivers from the old days and nothing missed him. He *had* to notice that cap. Suddenly, still far away, Bookie heard the pounding noise of a semi-trailer. One of Murdock's!

Slowly, the sound grew louder and then the broad beams of the headlamps cut by the window. With those lights went Bookie's hopes. But no! The semi-trailer had stopped. Now it was in reverse. That sweet, whining reverse gear! Bookie stopped straining and relaxed.

It was exactly thirty-eight seconds, by Bookie's count, before the door to the office opened and the light snapped on. There stood Latch, the cap in one hand and the inevitable nickel bar of candy in the other. That ugly, leathery face was as beautiful to Bookie as any Miss Atlantic City.

Latch sauntered into the room and his eyebrows raised. "Ah, a stag at bay." He indicated the silver badge bearing Bookie's license number which was pinned to the cap. "At last I know why you've been wearing this doo-dad. Just so my lights should pick it up. And my! Look at that lipstick. Beautiful, red lips must have put it there. Who kissed you? Old man Murdock?"

Bookie kicked out at Latch, forgetting his legs were tied, and the unbalanced chair tumbled backward to the floor. Latch pulled out a pocket knife, severed the ropes, and pulled off the scarf. Bookie lay on the floor, stretched out luxuriously as the blood pounded freely through his limbs.

FINALLY, BOOKIE stood up. "Have any trouble?"

"It was a clear road," responded Latch. "A guy outside that looks like a gunsel saw me but he didn't try anything. What's up?"

"I'll tell you later. Let's get out of here."

They stepped out into the corridor. The bouncer named Freddy was standing there but none of the others were around.

"Don't start anything," said Bookie, "or I'll perform a gunselectomy."

"Why should I start anything?" Freddy sounded surprised. "I'm doing fine. I'm prouda my station in life, bub."

Bookie and Latch walked out. Nobody tried to stop them. The small, halfton truck was still where Bookie had left it. Something was wrong and Bookie was worried. The whole thing was too easy. Why had Luigi Colombo let him get away from the Twittering Bird without a fight?"

"Give out, Bookie," said Latch. "What happened?"

"I'll tell you some other time because we've got to get away from here quick. Something stinks. That outfit saw me leave but they did nothing to stop me. It's not like them."

"But—"

"Go on. Get back to the terminal. I'll see you there later." Bookie sprinted for his small truck and drove away. He turned off the Post Road and made the short trip back to the Cook house. He had found the sedan but he still had to find the man who had driven it when it hit his truck. He had an idea where to look for that man, but there was no profit in talking up to Luigi Colombo on the subject— not alone. The next time he would be backed up when he visited Luigi.

As he approached his destination he could see several cars parked in front of the Cook house. The police from Homicide were still there, for he recognized one of the cars as theirs by the cop behind the wheel. He wondered, as he parked the truck and walked toward the house, if the Homicide cops had found Marcus Lunding.

On the front stoop sat Felton, looking worried. He drew a deep breath of relief at sight of Bookie and said: "I thought you were going to Murdock's Bridgeport terminal to report."

"I didn't have the chance," Bookie lied. "I had to stop off some place."

Felton wiped his forehead. "It's fortunate for me that you decided to come back." He looked sore. "And for you, too," he added. "I don't like to have a fast one put over on me."

"What's eating you, Felton?" Bookie asked. "Do you believe that redhead's crazy claim that I killed Amos Cook?"

Felton shook his head. "No. But she told the Homicide dick and he gave me hell for letting you go. Come on in and get me off this spot, Bookie."

Bookie said: "Lunding's the man they want. That business about me being beneficiary to his will is screwy. Lunding never saw me before tonight so he couldn't have named me in his will. A phone call to Lunding's lawyer will prove that, if necessary."

Felton said: "Come on inside and tell it to the Homicide dick."

Bookie followed the state cop into the living-room. The Homicide man was there with Susan Cook and a sleek young man that Bookie figured was Susan's brother, Frank.

There was a corpse there too. Another corpse. It lay on the floor and it was covered by a sheet but through the cloth Bookie could make out the sharp edges of the steel brace around the neck. This time no one would dispute Marcus Lunding's claim that he was dead. Marcus Lunding had been murdered at last.

Susan Cook saw Bookie and went to work. "Do you believe me now?" she screamed. "Does this man have to murder all of us before you police arrest him? He killed my father and my uncle because he wants the money that belongs to Frank and me. But he'll never get it! I'm going to fight him all the way!"

Bookie backed behind Felton and Frank Cook said: "Shut up, sis."

The Homicide detective seconded the suggestion and turned to Bookie. "Let's have it," he said.

"I didn't kill Marcus Lunding," Bookie said. "When I left here I went down to the Twittering Bird to find the sedan that crashed me and I found it. Colombo and his toughies tied me up. Latch, another truck driver, came along and got me out of it. Then I came here. If you don't believe me, Latch will back me up."

Felton said: "I know Latch. His truck passes here every night about this time."

"When did this Latch come along?" the Homicide cop said.

"About twenty minutes ago."

"Then Latch won't be good enough, Bookie." The cop looked at his watch. "Just about forty-seven minutes ago I heard a shot and ran outside to find Marcus Lunding dead, lying exactly as Amos Cook had been lying. Where were you then?"

"I was tied up at the Twittering Bird. And I can prove it. Latch found me there. And Colombo's singer, Margit, saw me. I got her to throw my cap with my license number out into the highway so that Latch, who was due along, would see it. This girl Margit probably can be made to talk even if Colombo and his toughies refuse to admit they tied me up. I had no reason to kill either Lunding or Cook. That business about me being named in Lunding's will is crazy. The guy never saw me before tonight. You can check on the will through Lunding's lawyer tomorrow."

"We're doing that now," the Homicide cop said. "But I've got to consider all angles. You might have been willing to gamble on the chance that Lunding had you in his will."

BOOKIE LAUGHED. "All I'm interested in is proving that the driver of that sedan was at fault when he hit my truck tonight, so I won't get docked my bonus for the next two years. And it looks as if I'll have to help find Cook's and Landing's killer to find the driver of that sedan."

The Homicide man said: "Well, you stick with me until I tell you otherwise. Come along. Let's go see Colombo."

The Homicide car stopped in front of the Henry Jason building and Bookie stepped from the back, followed by the watchful Homicide man. Luigi Colombo and the bouncer, Freddy, were lolling outside the door of the Twittering Bird and observed their approach with vast disinterest.

The cop said to Colombo: "I understand you're alibiing him, Luigi."

"Who's him?" asked Colombo.

"Bookie Barnes here. He claims he was inside your joint the last hour. Tied to a chair in your office. How about it?"

Luigi Colombo took his pleasantest smile off the shelf and used it. "It's not bad."

"What isn't?" asked the cop.

"The rib."

"This is no rib. We're serious," Felton put in.

"Sure, Felton, sure. But you should have tried it with some guy I knew," Colombo said. "I never saw this Bookie Barnes in my life."

Bookie felt a sinking feeling in his stomach. He was beginning, too, to understand why Colombo had let him escape. Colombo knew that Marcus Lunding had been killed. He had let Bookie escape so as to rig him for the job. A frame, pure and not so simple.

A door to the night club opened and one of the customers came out. Behind the threshold, for the moment the door was open, Bookie saw Margit Otvos. She glanced at him without recognition. So she was in on it too!

"Wait a second." Bookie tried to keep calm as he leveled a finger at the bouncer. "You. You saw me come out. You know when I came in and when I left here. You helped tie me up."

Freddy grew thoughtful, then snapped his fingers. "Say," he exclaimed, "I think I did lamp a couple of guys in windbreakers walk out of the office. I thought they were delivering something. But that was more than an hour ago."

The Homicide man shook his head. "It's not good enough, Bookie. I'm sorry about it. I guess the thought of all that dough just drove you berserker."

"What are you talking about? Can't you see this is a frame? You—" Bookie suddenly remembered Henry Jason. "Come on. I've got somebody else to alibi me. And he's good."

He grabbed the Homicide man's arm and dragged him around to the main entrance of the building, Felton trailing them. As they climbed the steps to the first floor, Bookie could hear a phone ring from where Jason's office was located. He swore. Luigi Colombo was undoubtedly letting Henry Jason in on the frame, if he hadn't already.

They pushed open the door to Jason's office. Jason looked up from behind his desk, pencil in hand, and said: "Yes?"

"Who phoned you just now?" Bookie said.

"I beg your pardon?" Jason looked blank.

"We heard the phone ring as we came up the stairs. Colombo was tipping you off not to recognize me. I suppose you'll claim I wasn't up here an hour ago."

"A half truth," murmured Henry Jason. "The phone did ring, but in the next office. However, it's true that I've never before seen you."

The Homicide man pushed Bookie towards the door. "It's no use, Bookie. We'll check on the stories you think up later. You're wasting my time. You can't stall us forever. I'm running you in."

Bookie decided he didn't like the way things were going. Desperately he grasped at straws. "Has that kid, Frank Cook, got an alibi?" he said.

"We'll find that out too. Meanwhile, you aren't impressing me with this kind of stuff, Bookie."

Bookie said: "All right. But will you remember to check with Marcus Lunding's lawyer on that will?"

"Sure. Anything to make you happy."

Felton had gone on ahead of them and Bookie could hear him going through the door to the street down the one flight of stairs. Bookie and the Homicide man were alone in the corridor.

Bookie said, "Don't forget," and brought up his right fist. It was an imposing fist, square with heavy knuckles. The Homicide cop's head snapped back and he slumped to the ground.

Bookie paused long enough to feel the cop's jaw. There seemed to be no fracture and he hurried downstairs, peered out into the street. Colombo and his bouncer had, apparently, gone inside the night club. The cop chauffeuring the department car was facing the other way, and Felton was not in sight.

Bookie stole a few hundred feet beyond the Jason building, then crossed the Post Road. He saw a semi-trailer approaching, recognized it as one of Murdock's jobs. When it came abreast of him, he jumped on the running board.

Mike Projak was at the wheel and Bookie said to him: "Keep going. I'm a dangerous guy, Mike. I've killed two men already tonight."

CHAPTER FIVE
AND HEAVY FISTS

BOOKIE BARNES sat on a crate in the trailer. The semi-trailer was parked just outside Bridgeport by a lunch wagon the boys called the Stink House. He had told Mike Projak enough to prevail on him to park by the wagon while he tried to think himself out of his jam.

He knew that his story was making the rounds of the drivers and that by morning it would be known from Boston to Philly but he wasn't worried. He knew also that no one would turn him in, that if such a thought occurred to anyone he would be deterred by sheer fear of the other drivers. A little while before, sirens had sounded on the Post Road and he had changed over to a National trailer also parked outside the Stink House. But the cops had just looked into the lunch wagon without bothering to search the trucks.

However, he was not thinking himself out of his jam too successfully. He was sure of only one thing—that he had no intention of being booked on a murder charge. He knew he could probably beat the charge in the long run but that would mean time and lawyers and money. And now the cops wouldn't be bearing him any good will.

A driver reached in and handed Bookie a cup of steaming coffee. He took it without bothering to see who it was and again searched over the slender threads of reason he could see in the case. The sedan and the wrecked truck seemed unimportant now. The paramount thing was to find someone upon whom to hang the killings. There were too many candidates.

The Svengali had been wrong on one count. It was not Amos Cook who had shoved Marcus Lunding off a cliff, breaking his neck. That was as certain as that it was *not* Lunding who had murdered his brother-in-law. Either Frank or Susan Cook might have killed Lunding to get his money. Luigi Colombo might have killed Lunding because his business was being ruined by Lunding's reformist activities. The same reason held for Henry Jason.

But those were motives to kill the Svengali, not Amos Cook.

The trailer door swung open and Latch jumped in. "I heard you were loused up, Bookie."

"Uh-huh," said Bookie absently. He sipped the coffee and wondered what single motive could have impelled the murders of both Amos Cook and Marcus Lunding.

"If it's real bad," persisted Latch, "we can figure out a route and get you out to the West coast or the Mex border by slow stages."

"Go away."

"All right, but you shouldn't hit cops. By the way, there's some punk in the Stink House asking after you. What'll we tell him?"

"What punk?" asked Bookie.

"He says his name is Frank Cook and he's trying to find you. Do we kick him out or what?"

"Bring him here," said Bookie after some hesitation. It could be a trap but he was in no position to be choosy.

Latch left and reappeared a few moments later with Frank Cook. Bookie trained his flashlight on Marcus Lunding's nephew. He had a petulant, spoiled face, one that could show no determination unless it was faced with some honest labor. Margit Otvos had been right about one thing. There was too much vaseline on the hair.

"How did you know where to find me?" asked Bookie.

"I heard how you got away from the cops," Frank Cook replied, "and I started hunting for you along the Road in the places where truck drivers hang out."

"Why?"

"I didn't want there to be any hard feelings, Mr. Barnes. Susan was just excited before. She didn't really mean what she was saying."

"You're very kind," murmured Bookie and waited to hear the real reason for the visit.

"To tell you the truth," Frank Cook finally blurted, "I was afraid my sister might have queered everything by yelling about that will."

"Don't tell me you also believe that business about your uncle leaving me all his dough."

"Of course not, Mr. Barnes. I just didn't want that to queer it because if we stick together there'll be plenty for both of us."

Bookie's frown slowly melted into a grin. Everything had clicked into place. He knew the answer now.

He turned the flash on his watch dial as Frank Cook talked. Two thirty. Luigi Colombo would still be there, counting up the night's receipts without having to take off

his shoes. "Let's begin," he said to Latch. "Go in the Stink
House and tell the boys to come along."

"I DON'T want to get into any trouble, Mr. Barnes."

Frank Cook said it and Bookie Barnes did not reply
immediately. He looked out through the moving trailer's
rear doors and could count five trucks following them
down the Boston Post Road. There were some nine of
them, excluding the vaselined punk, and that was just sufficient to welcome the night club owner.

"Just keep quiet and come along with us," Bookie finally
said, "or you'll be in for plenty of trouble."

A few minutes later, the six mammoth trucks stopped
in front of the Henry Jason building and the drivers piled
out. Pulling the reluctant Frank Cook with him, Bookie
jumped down.

The Twittering Bird's signs were dark and the front door
locked. The lock on the door was not quite good enough
to withstand the heavy shoulders ramming against it and
soon the catch snapped and they broke into the night
club's corridor.

Luigi Colombo must have heard the trucks approaching
for a reception committee was waiting. Colombo and his
men—bouncers, waiters, cooks, musicians—were lined up
in a heavy mass. Over twenty of them, armed with cleavers
and bats, against the nine drivers equipped mostly with
jack handles or crowbars.

Freddy's hand dug into a pocket and came up with his
gun. Bookie hurled the flashlight he carried, catching the
bouncer over the bridge of the nose. The drivers took it as
their signal and surged forward.

The truckmen fought with gusto. Big or small, clumsy or
agile, they were trained on heavy work—wrestling crates

or lifting loads often beyond their strength. Few of them fought with any pretense to science, accepting a dozen blows before delivering one. But that one was executed with ponderous, heavy efficiency and rarely required a follow-up.

Bats and cleavers were disposed of with the jack handles and, in one case, with a jack itself. Then weapons were dropped in favor of heavy, block fists. Rapidly, Colombo's men fell back and it was not long before the help dived for the shelter of tables or booths to lick wounds, leaving the bouncers to face the drivers.

Bookie found himself dodging Luigi Colombo. The ex-bootlegger knew how to fight and Bookie could already feel the swelling mouse over his left eye. He moved in to get a stinging blow on his jaw before Colombo danced out of his reach. Enraged, Bookie stopped boxing and threw himself forward like a halfback, bearing the night club owner to the ground. He sat on top of Colombo and his fist chopped down once. Colombo stopped struggling.

Feet raced by and Bookie could see one of the truck drivers chasing after a waiter. "Let him go," he yelled.

"He'll phone the cops if he gets out!"

"That's what I want."

Everything was suddenly quiet. Those of the Twittering Bird had had enough of truckmen. There was a peal of delighted laughter. Margit Otvos sat on the bar, legs swinging. "Admirably done, sugar."

The drivers corralled Colombo and his bouncers and herded them into the office. The rest were ignored.

Bookie called to Mike Projak. "Go up to the first floor and bring down Henry Jason. He'll be sitting at his desk, figuring numbers and looking very important."

THE BOUNCERS lay on the floor, their noses buried in the carpet. If they moved, a kick in the ribs from one of the drivers was sufficient to still them. Luigi Colombo and Henry Jason sat very quietly in chairs and Frank Cook, looking very unhappy, had his back pressed in a corner as if he were trying to disappear through it. Only Margit Otvos, sitting on the desk top with legs curled under her, appeared gay and unworried.

"The cops will be around soon," Bookie said to her. "Are you willing to tell them I was tied up in here when Marcus Lunding was murdered?"

"I'm sorree." She nodded to Colombo. "He pays my salary and you are only still a truck driver."

Bookie turned to the night club owner. "Then will you admit you had me here during that time?"

"Go strip your gear, brother."

"You'll change your mind. Where's that jack?" Bookie's eyes fell on the radiator. An end was two feet away from one of the walls. "That'll be perfect."

Luigi Colombo said: "If you're thinking of squeezing my arm or leg with that jack you're—"

"I'm what," asked Bookie, "because I'm thinking of it?"

The night club owner shrugged. "Then you're on the right track, Bookie, because it ain't worth it to me. Sure you were here when Marcus Lunding was killed."

"You could have saved yourself a lot of trouble," Bookie said, "by not trying to frame me."

For the first time, Henry Jason spoke. "I'll admit it too, Barnes," Jason said. "We were just trying to teach you a lesson, so don't start figuring it proves any of us did the murders."

"My figuring is doing fine," replied Bookie, "ever since Frank Cook offered to split with me. And he wasn't talking about his uncle's will either."

They could hear the squeal of police car brakes, traveling without sirens, as they pulled up in front of the Jason building and a moment later the Homicide man, heading a contingent of cops, burst into the room. The Homicide cop's jaw was taped.

Bookie spoke hurriedly.

"I'll make a deal with you—"

The Homicide man yelled: "You crazy killer! The only deal you're making with me is in the back room."

"You're making a fool of yourself, pal," said Bookie. "This bunch has already admitted I was here, the way I claimed, when Marcus Lunding was murdered."

The cop hesitated. "Is that so?" he asked Colombo as if he hoped it wasn't.

"The hell with that kind of cheesy lying," said the night club owner. "Sure he was here."

"I too saw him here," added Margit brightly.

The Homicide man glowered around the room. He glanced suspiciously at the recumbent hoods and the drivers and put away the revolver. "Then why the hell did you deny it in the first place?"

Colombo was silent and Bookie said: "They wanted to pin the killings on me."

"I know why I'd want you to burn but why should they?" the cop growled.

"Because they knew that if they didn't deliver a first-class suspect then they themselves would be on the carpet."

"It still doesn't give you any call to hit a policeman."

"That's the deal I want to make with you," Bookie said. "Forget that sock and I'll give you your murderer."

The cop stood uncertainly for a moment, then grunted acquiescence. "I'm not promising anything but let's hear."

"Well, it begins some time ago with Marcus Lunding. He was one of those pillars of society who fight sin and use soap for a toothpaste. He also had dough and he had the idea that Amos Cook, his brother-in-law, and Frank and Susan were willing to murder him for it. His idea was probably correct but that wasn't why someone finally did kill him."

"Leave me out of this," interrupted Colombo. "I was here all night and my boys can back it up."

"You were here with me," said Margit Otvos with the hint of a threat.

"And I was in my office upstairs," Henry Jason thought it necessary to say.

Frank Cook tried to speak but only a frightened whine resulted.

"None of which proves anything," said the Homicide man. "Go on, Barnes."

BOOKIE CONTINUED: "Marcus Lunding so feared for his life that he went to his summer home to hide out. But the killer followed him and shoved him off a cliff. The fall broke his neck but Lunding didn't die. Tonight Lunding came back here with every intention of murdering the Cooks who he believed tried to kill him to get his money. On the way, Lunding had me stop the truck while he made a phone call. He told me he phoned Amos Cook that he was on the way to kill him.

"As a result of that phone call, the murderer tried to beat Lunding to the punch by wrecking my truck. At first

I figured it was Amos Cook that crashed my truck. But I know now that Cook was not the killer. I know too that it was not Lunding who killed Amos Cook. Lunding never got a chance to kill Cook."

"What are you getting at?" Henry Jason broke in impatiently.

"Me," said Luigi Colombo. "He thinks I had a motive to kill both Cook and Lunding on account of that lousy mission Lunding built next door to ruin my business. But he's wrong. All I ever did was try to scare Lunding out of ruining my business by sending my boys over."

"That's right," Bookie agreed. "You had reason to kill Marcus Lunding, but not Amos Cook." He turned to Frank Cook. "How far is it, kid?"

"Twenty-four inches," Frank said.

"Cut the doubletalk," snapped the Homicide cop. "What's this business about twenty-four inches?"

"It has to do with this building," Bookie said. "And it's the reason why both Amos Cook and Lunding were murdered. Henry Jason owns this lot on which the Jason Building stands—all except two feet of it. Marcus Lunding owned that two feet, plus the land next door on which he erected the mission. Jason hired Amos Cook to design and build this building. Before the building was completed Amos quit the job. Why? He said it was because Jason wasn't paying him for his work.

"About this time Margit Otvos began trying to get into Lunding's good graces."

"Why?" Margit said.

"You were trying to talk Lunding into selling Jason two feet of land from that property next door. Jason told you that he wanted to build a fence on that land, a fence high enough to hide that mission. But that isn't so because Henry Jason didn't really care if he was forced to put Colombo's night club out of the building—he can always rent this space to some other business and make the same money out of it. The truth is that Jason tried to get Lunding to make a deal—Jason told Lunding that he would cancel Colombo's contract, get rid of the night club, provided Marcus Lunding would sell Henry Jason two feet of land next door."

"What the hell good would two feet of land do him?" the Homicide cop asked.

Bookie said: "That two feet of land—just twenty-four inches—is underneath the Jason Building. Amos Cook deliberately ran the Jason Building over onto two feet of Marcus Lunding's land. Amos knew that when Lunding found out about it there would be a fight between Jason and Lunding. Amos knew that Marcus Lunding had cut the Cook family out of his will. Amos decided to kill Lunding, and at the same time fix up a blackmailing setup that would get him some money—some of Henry Jason's money.

"Amos Cook deliberately extended the Jason building over two feet of Lunding's property to start a feud between Jason and Marcus Lunding. When Lunding was murdered, Cook would threaten to tell the police that Lunding and Jason had fought about that two feet of Lunding's land, which Jason had tried to buy and Lunding had refused to sell. Lunding's lawyer would know about that, would be a witness. And Jason would have trouble proving that he didn't kill Marcus Lunding. Amos Cook meant to see to that.

"Amos Cook quit his job with Jason before the building was finished so that later he could say that he had quit when he found out the building was partly on his uncle Lunding's land."

Bookie looked at Henry Jason who sat in his chair, tense and motionless.

"It was a good blackmail scheme. Amos Cook could collect money indefinitely from Jason to keep quiet about that two feet of Lunding's land. To move a building the size of the Jason Building would cost a fortune, if possible at all."

"We checked with Lunding's lawyer," the Homicide man said. "I got word by phone just before we came here that the land next door is being willed to a church and Lunding's dough goes to charities."

Bookie nodded. "And Amos Cook knew it. Amos was smart. But he didn't figure that Henry Jason would fight his blackmail scheme the way he did—by killing both Amos and Lunding."

HENRY JASON stood up abruptly, like an automaton. His face was white, lifeless. He stared at Bookie Barnes with expressionless eyes, but he did not speak. Felton reached for Jason's arm, held him fast.

The Homicide cop said: "How do you know all this, Bookie?"

"Some of it I figured. But I got the blackmail setup from Frank Cook. When Frank heard that story about Lunding leaving *me* his money, Frank believed it. So he propositioned me. Said he wouldn't contest the will if I would make it possible for him to continue blackmailing Jason. Frank had been in on his father's scheme, of course."

Henry Jason's eyes turned to Frank Cook's cringing weak face, and expression came to them for the first time. "Yes," Jason said through his colorless lips. "Yes, he was in on it.

He and his father meant to ruin me, to bleed me dry. They knew I was at Marcus Lunding's summer home when they tried to kill him. They told me to go there, to talk with Lunding about selling me that two feet of land. They framed me. But they failed to kill old Lunding that time. I knew they'd try again—and succeed eventually. And I was helpless to stop them because they could show that I had been fighting with old Lunding about that land. And the fact that they were not to inherit Lunding's property would clear them…."

Bookie sighed, started for the door. Margit Otvos reached out and rumpled his hair as he passed the desk.

"Threeling work, sugar."

He looked her over. "Maybe we'll have a date tomorrow night."

"On a truck driver's salary, pet?" Bookie grinned at her. "Lucky me," he said.

DANCE MACABRE

THERE WAS NOTHING TOO
TOUGH FOR THAT LITTLE LUNGER
TO TAKE—EVEN ACTING AS A
WALKING CHECKROOM FOR A
GUNSEL'S GAT—SO LONG AS HE
COULD BE NEAR HIS THREE-FOR-
A-DIME DANCE-HALL MOUSE. AND
THE NIGHT SHE WAS SHIVED
THERE WAS NOTHING LEFT FOR
HIM TO DO BUT CASH IN THE LIFE
HE'D BEEN HOARDING—TO SETTLE
THE SCORE WITH HER KILLER.

CHAPTER ONE
SWOLLEN FEET

OUTSIDE, THE neon sign styled Jugger Callahan as the *King of Swing* but since Jugger owned the Tango Palace and had conferred the title on himself, not many people believed it. The sign also described the forty-eight hostesses as glorious, glittering, glamorous, and *that*, absolutely nobody believed—not even the girls.

Inside, Jugger Callahan kicked off the beat to the *Smiling Troubadours*. They played mechanically, with that automatic, pounding, unvarying rhythm that experienced jazz bands acquire, and, belying their name, they were unsmiling. It was nearing the closing hour of one A.M. and they were tired.

The tinted baby spots that were set in the ceiling revolved and played amber, red and blue over the dance floor. The place was large and ramshackle—the kind of second-story loft where you get natty, credit clothing—and it was just as much a fire trap as the taxi joint that had burned down on Jugger two months before. Nevertheless, the Tango Palace was a thriving enterprise aiming at that thin item of change known as the "dime." The dances were three for a dime and most of the customers stayed on a dime through all three of them.

The hostesses who waited for trade, chatted behind the frayed velvet rope that encircled the dance floor. Their

low-cut evening gowns were creased and soiled, their eyes heavy-lidded with mascara and no sleep. Yet when a customer seemed inclined to switch partners, smiles appeared on vermilion lips, hips undulated sensuously and swollen, tired feet suggestively beat time to the music. Out of every dime ticket theirs was two and a half cents.

Ephraim Tuttle, who served as business manager, accountant and general factotum for Jugger Callahan, wandered back and forth, keeping a nervous eye on the girls and the ticket chopper. He was a tall, gaunt man with a bony skeleton-face. His treatment of the girls was always scrupulously fair and they respected him. They could not even accuse him of showing favoritism to Evelyn Dorn, his flame of the moment.

He made a mental calculation of the swaying couples on the dance floor and found that business was only fair

Rocco whipped out his handkerchief and carefully wiped the gun.

for a Friday night. He decided that they'd better pass out some more handbills on Spring and Main streets and approached a man quietly sitting on one of the settees that lined a wall.

"Firpo, have you been messing around in my office?"

Firpo Cole looked up at Ephraim Tuttle. "No. Why should I?"

"Someone stole my letter opener," responded Tuttle.

"That's bad," said Firpo. "If you get a letter now you'll have to open it with your fingers."

Ephraim Tuttle pulled a five-cent stogie out of his vest, carefully split the end and lit it before replying. "It's funny," he mused, "how the squirts always act the toughest. If I'd spit at you you'd drown, yet you like to throw your weight around."

"Just leave me alone," said Firpo. "When somebody loses a night's sleep around here they right away think I took it."

"Firpo, you don't appreciate the break we're giving you. We let you mooch a few bucks around here instead of letting you go back to picking pockets on the street. But remember, it's only because Ruth Bailey's a nice girl and she wants us to give you a break."

"Thanks."

"I don't know what you want from the Bailey kid anyway, Firpo. You'll never get to first base and—"

Ephraim Tuttle broke off as he noticed Firpo Cole's face. He didn't like what he saw there. "God, but you're touchy about that skirt," he muttered and walked away.

With expressionless eyes, Firpo Cole watched the business manager retreat. He didn't know that his face, which always showed an unhealthy pallor, was now even whiter and more strained than usual. He was a youngish, frail man with spindle-legs, chicken-breast and sunken cheeks, and he had once been facetiously dubbed "Firpo" by someone who was supposed to be as funny as a card.

He found a loose cigarette in his pocket and lit it. As he did so, he forgot to make his customary salute to the medical profession by thumbing his nose. The medicos had told him that each cigarette took one month of his life. Like oil and water, cigarettes and lungs don't mix.

Jugger Callahan and his boys wound up the quickie trio of dances and immediately started on another set of three. The hostesses collected tickets from the men and slipped into their arms for another few minutes of those curious, swaying gyrations that passed for dancing.

Firpo Cole took a pad out of his pocket and marked down the figure 8. Then he leaned back to watch a man and a girl sitting and talking on a sofa in a far corner. He didn't like to have Ruth Bailey sitting out dances. It was a funny thing, he reflected, but he didn't at all mind when Ruth Bailey was being pawed by some ten-dollar millionaire out on the floor. It was her job. At first, his stomach used to tighten up from jealousy but even that had stopped. You get used to those things. What he did mind, though, was to have her talking with some man through eight dances and not get the tickets for them. She was an easy mark for chiselers. But he'd see to it that this baby got away with nothing. He could do nothing if Ruth preferred some other guy to him, but at least he'd see to it she wasn't rooked out of her rights.

ON THE band platform, Jugger Callahan broke into *Ain't Misbehavin'* and Mona Leeds, the outfit's torch singer, took over the mike. A hush settled over the place. The voice was rich and husky and, like her face and figure, possessed a torrid beauty. She sang into the mike but faced Jugger Callahan—as if to let the world know who her man was.

Mona Leeds finished her number and the dance hall echoed with appreciative whistles and stomping feet. Next to Firpo Cole, a voice said: "That's the kind of chicken they should have in every pot."

Firpo looked up to find Rocco Pace standing beside him. Rocco was one of the city's moderately successful racketeers. He dressed according to color charts, seemed pleasant and mild-mannered, but, if occasion demanded, could be dangerous.

Firpo said: "Yeah, Mona's all right."

Rocco nodded toward Ruth Bailey who still talked with the stranger. "But nothing like her, eh?"

"Nobody's like her," said Firpo in a flat, emotionless voice.

"Has she still got that yen for Jugger?"

Firpo Cole nodded.

"How come you take it laying down, Firpo? Me, I'd blow a fuse."

"Jugger's a good-looking guy. I don't blame her. I'm just going to see she gets them dealt from the top of the deck."

Rocco Pace shrugged. Certain things were beyond his Latin comprehension. He slipped a flat .32 automatic out of a shoulder holster and handed it to Firpo Cole who dropped it in his pocket. It was a service for which Firpo usually made four bits. Rocco had long ago discovered that he couldn't hold the girls the way he liked if he sported an eighteen-ounce piece of metal over his chest.

Rocco Pace waved to Firpo and walked toward the barrier. The hostesses made a beeline for him. They liked this smiling, pleasant racketeer who gave big tips and who really came to dance.

Firpo Cole saw the stranger in the corner stand up and nod a farewell to Ruth Bailey. He didn't hand her any tickets. Firpo waited till the man got near him, then stood up and blocked his path.

"Well?" asked the stranger. He was middle-aged and asthmatic.

Firpo Cole said: "What are you trying to get away with?"

"Anything I can," replied the stranger pleasantly.

"Well, I'm here to see that you don't, mister."

"Get out of my way, son."

"Not till you pay her, chiseler."

"Pay Miss Bailey?" The stranger sounded puzzled. "Maybe you got me mixed up with Santa Claus."

"You owe her ten tickets," said Firpo, figuring the extra two as a tip. "That'll be one buck."

"For the last time, get out of my way."

Firpo Cole knew it was coming but he did nothing to prevent it. Ruth Bailey was worth a beating any day in the week. It never occurred to him to draw the flat automatic in his pocket.

The stranger's arm came around in a wide arc that sent the frail Firpo spinning over the floor for fifteen feet. Firpo saw the stranger leave with unhurried steps, then a sudden attack of vertigo seized him and he passed out.

FIRPO COLE came to on a couch in Ephraim Tuttle's office. Mona Leeds, the torch singer, was swabbing his forehead with a damp rag and, from behind his desk, the business manager regarded them sourly.

Tuttle said: "Firpo, for a guy who couldn't lick a butterfly you certainly like to throw your weight around."

"Stop riding him," snapped Mona Leeds.

The door opened and Ruth Bailey came in. "Firpo, they told me you were in a fight. Are you all right?"

Firpo Cole struggled into a sitting posture. "Nothing happened. I'm fine."

Ruth seemed to notice the torch singer for the first time. The corners of her mouth twisted. "Well, well, if it isn't our little thrush trying to cut in on Firpo."

"Now, Ruth," said Firpo weakly. "She was just trying to help me."

Mona Leeds stood up and walked over to the hostess. The two women faced each other: Mona Leeds, in all her beautiful, slithering, scented allure, and Ruth Bailey, refreshing and young in a simple gown with a gold brooch at the neck. The one, a night life beauty with a duco finish, the other, a breath of fresh air too rare in a taxi-joint.

Ruth Bailey's voice had a faint hint of hysteria. "Why aren't you satisfied with Jugger? You got him solid—why do you want more? Firpo would be a pretty miserable addition to your collection. Why don't you leave him alone?"

"You ———," said the torch singer.

Ruth's hand snapped out and slapped Mona Leeds squarely over the face.

Ephraim Tuttle's warning shout was lost as the torch singer sprang for Ruth Bailey, her claws spread like a cat's. Mona's hands tore into Ruth's face and hair and the hostess clutched at the singer's dress. In a moment they were on the floor, scrabbling in mute fury. Paralyzed with the fascination of the spectacle, the two men simply watched.

With a yank, Ruth ripped apart the front of Mona's dress and the torch singer sank sharp, white, translucent teeth into the hostess's shoulder. Long, lacquered nails clawed, fists pummeled, slipper-shod feet kicked. The wildcats rolled over the floor and, with squeals of rage, tore at hair, face, clothing.

The door opened and Rocco Pace appeared. He said, "What the hell," and leaped to separate the fighting girls.

Their fury subsided as suddenly as it rose and they stood up, appraising the damage they had done each other.

"That's a lousy way to act in my office," complained Ephraim Tuttle.

"Oh go add up some numbers," said Mona Leeds calmly. She pulled her torn dress together and left.

Ruth Bailey anxiously scanned her face in a compact mirror.

"Girls will be girls," philosophized the racketeer. "I used to have one who tried to kill me every time I went to sleep."

Ruth Bailey picked up the brooch that had been ripped from her gown. It was a simple item of jewelry, with what seemed to be a pale-blue piece of glass set in the center.

"Say, don't that belong to Mona?" asked Tuttle.

"Even if it did," replied Ruth Bailey smoothly, "I wouldn't give it to her." Then she walked out.

"There's life in those girls," said Rocco Pace. He turned to Firpo Cole. "I came for my persuader."

Firpo returned the automatic. The racketeer tossed him a half dollar and bade them good-bye.

Tuttle snorted and hunted for a cigar. "This place is getting to be a regular nuthouse. First somebody steals my letter opener and now this. Did you hook that opener, Firpo?"

Firpo Cole was feeling a little better. The stranger hadn't hit him very hard. He said: "Don't bother me."

Ephraim Tuttle's Adam's apple bobbed up and down. "Listen, you lousy pickpocket, I'm just asking nicely if you took it. It was pretty valuable. It had an onyx handle with silver edging."

Firpo said, "The hell with you and your letter opener," got up and left.

IT WAS after one already and the customers had gone. On the bandstand, Jugger Callahan and his boys were putting away their instruments, though Monkey Harris, a drummer, still banged on the skins as if to relieve his pent-up weariness.

Firpo Cole made his way to the back, entered a large dressing-room and sat down in a corner to wait for Ruth Bailey. The hostesses were hanging their gowns in a closet and changing into street clothes. Some sat quietly and rested their swollen feet in pans of hot water. None paid the slightest attention to Firpo.

Ruth Bailey changed her stockings, which had snagged during the fight, and touched up a blackened eye with powder. Ephraim Tuttle came in and asked whether anyone had seen his letter opener. No one had and he left. Ruth Bailey finished making up and she and Firpo Cole quit the dressing-room and went out to the street.

These nightly walks, when he took her home, were usually full with the talk and gossip of the Tango Palace, but tonight, it was some time before Ruth Bailey finally broke the heavy silence between them.

"Firpo, I'm afraid."

"Forget it, Ruth. Mona won't get you fired. She's too white for that."

"I'm not talking about the fight," she said. "I just forgot myself when I saw her by you and she was mad about this." She touched the brooch at her throat.

"What has that got to do with it?"

"Well, you remember the night the old ballroom burned down? I went back for my purse which I'd forgotten and there was a light in Jugger's office. I went inside and there was no one there but I saw a jewel case on his desk. It had this inside of it."

"You shouldn't of taken it."

"Maybe, but all I knew was that Jugger bought it for Mona and I guess I got jealous. I started wearing it a few days ago. Jugger's seen it but he's too much of a gentleman to say anything. But Mona knows it belongs to her and that's what she was really fighting about with me."

"You've got to give it to her, Ruth."

"I will. Tomorrow. She's beautiful—I don't blame Jugger for preferring her to me."

"Jugger may be a nice guy but he's a damned fool for wanting Mona Leeds instead of you."

They reached her rooming house and halted.

"You know, Firpo, it's funny how I'm sick about Jugger and you about me. It seems like such a damned shame that life never—"

"I know all about it," he cut in harshly. "You didn't tell me what you're afraid of."

"Firpo, someone—I don't know who—put five hundred dollars in my purse tonight."

He whistled. "That's a lot of money."

She reached into her coat pocket. "This is what the money came in."

He took a plain, white envelope from her hand and read the typewritten line on it: *This better be enough.*

Under a lamplight, Firpo Cole's prematurely weazened face was lost in thought. After a while he returned the envelope to her and said: "You better hold on to this and the dough. You didn't see anyone messing around with your purse tonight?"

"No—but of course anyone could have gotten at it in the dressing-room."

"Has anything like this happened before?"

"No."

"Well, all I can figure, Ruth, is that someone's mixing you up with somebody else. I'll try and check tomorrow."

"There's another thing, Firpo. You know that man you had a fight with today?"

"What about him?"

"He said not to tell anybody but he's a detective from an insurance company. They think that fire wasn't an accident. He knows I came back that night after everyone was gone and he asked me a lot of questions about it."

Firpo Cole shrugged. "If that fire's faked it's Jugger's worry—not yours. He got the insurance dough from it."

"I know Jugger wouldn't do a thing like that. Something's wrong, Firpo. I'm afraid."

"Forget it, Ruth."

She leaned over and kissed him full on the lips. "You're swell, Firpo. I'm sorry we don't hit it off together."

"Sure," said Firpo Cole. "I'm swell." He turned abruptly and made for his own lodgings.

CHAPTER TWO
DEAD FEET

THERE WAS hard and insistent rapping on the door panel. After some time, the steady pounding had its effect. Firpo Cole stirred uneasily in his sleep, then awoke with a start.

He groped for the light chain above his bed and the light revealed a small, unkempt, five-dollar-a-week room. He knuckled his eyes, then peered at a clock on the dresser but found that he had forgotten to wind it. Through the window he could see the first streaks of dawn. The pounding on the door did not let up.

Firpo Cole disentangled himself from the bed covers, worked his feet into straw slippers and opened the door. Two men entered. He knew one—a plainclothes police dick named Simms. The other was a uniformed cop.

Simms said, "Go to it, Max," and the uniformed cop began a somewhat perfunctory search of the room. The dick sat down on the bed. "How you getting along, Firpo?"

"Fine," replied Firpo Cole. "And you?"

"Just dandy, thanks. Have you been picking pockets lately, Firpo?"

"No."

"That's swell. Your record ain't so good on the blotter, is it?"

"I lost once."

"I remember, Firpo. Meatball rap. Two years in college, wasn't it?"

"One year. What is this, Simms—a frame?"

The police dick shook his head. "Nope. I've just been checking on you, Firpo. I'm glad you're going straight. What time did you check in last night?"

"I came home around two or a little after."

"Go out again?"

"No."

"How do you pay for your room and grits, Firpo?"

"I do odd jobs around the Tango Palace."

Simms nodded sagely. "So I hear. I also hear you're carrying a torch for one of the dames that works there—a Ruth Bailey—and that she won't give you a tumble because she got a yen for Jugger Callahan."

"What are you driving at, Simms?"

Max was finished with his cursory examination of the room. "Nothing," he grunted.

Simms shrugged. "There's nothing to find anyway. It's open and shut." He turned to Firpo again. "I'll tell you what I'm driving at. That Ruth Bailey of yours was murdered a couple of hours ago."

"If you're being funny," said Firpo Cole tonelessly, "I'll kill you, Simms."

Simms said: "Sure I'm being funny. Me and Max come here only to have tea and crumpets."

Firpo's eyes searched the police dick's face. He saw that Simms was speaking the truth. Suddenly he felt sick. He got up and stumbled through the door, across the hallway, to the washroom. He kneeled over the bowl and the flesh-less body shook and strained convulsively.

Simms cautioned, "Don't let the guy pull any fast one," and Max walked over to the open door and watched till Firpo returned.

Simms said: "I figure it this way, Firpo. Tell me if I get the details wrong. You were after Ruth Bailey but there was no sale because she was hot for this Jugger Callahan. So you got fed up with the whole business and went and killed her."

"I didn't kill her." He began to tremble and a fit of cough-ing seized him. He covered his mouth with a towel and when he took it away there were flecks of blood on it. "I didn't kill her," he repeated.

Simms said: "It probably just slipped your mind, Firpo. I guess we can make you remember again. Get some duds on that gorgeous torso of yours and come along."

THE PROWL car stopped at the rooming house of the late Ruth Bailey. The sun was already showing itself and supplanting the coolness of a Los Angeles night with a dry desert heat.

Simms, Max and Firpo Cole went up the two flights of groaning steps and entered Ruth Bailey's small apartment. The place had already been dusted and photoed and the few department men who remained sat around yawning and wishing they were home in bed. A couple of bored reporters were handicapping the Caliente races and exhibiting a complete disinterest in this murder of a taxi dance hall hostess.

The body lay on the floor where it had fallen. Simms yanked off the bed sheet that covered it and said: "Come here."

Firpo Cole walked over and stared down on Ruth Bailey. He thought he would be sick again but the feeling passed. She wore the same dress, and the brooch that Jugger had bought for Mona Leeds was still clasped at her neck. The steel point of Ephraim Tuttle's stolen letter opener was buried deep in her heart.

But Firpo was looking neither at the brooch nor the murder weapon. His eyes were fastened on the dead lips and the heavy coloring of lipstick over them—and on the strange shading of tangerine.

As if from a great distance, Firpo heard Simms' matter-of-fact voice saying: "Take a good look at what you done and then see if you still got the crust to deny it."

Firpo Cole gave a queer, strangled gasp and sank down on his knees beside the body. His hand went out and caressed Ruth Bailey's neck and he bent over and kissed her on the forehead. Behind him, a flashlight bulb exploded.

After a while, Firpo stood up. His eyes were dry and had a strange glint of understanding in them and the white, unhealthy face was set with rocky determination.

Simms said: "You did a pretty messy job, didn't you? Do you feel like talking about it now?"

"I didn't do it."

"No? Then who did?"

Firpo Cole was sure he knew. Jugger Callahan! It couldn't be anyone else. But his face gave no inkling of his thought. He would get at the truth—and when he did, no one but he would have the pleasure of dealing with the murderer. He said: "I didn't do this, Simms. I would of killed myself for even thinking of doing it."

Max gave a yell and pointed at the body. "It's gone!"

They followed the cop's fingers. The brooch that had been clasped at Ruth Bailey's neck was missing.

"Kee-rist!" roared Simms. "You lousy pickpocket, what the hell do you think you're pulling off here?"

The police dick grabbed at Firpo Cole and began to bounce him up and down like a cocktail shaker. "You wouldn't kill her!" he shouted. "Why you even rob her dead body to get a two buck hunk of jewelry!"

"I didn't take it," Firpo gasped as well as he could.

"No one else was near her," snorted Simms. His hands plunged into Firpo's pockets—and came up empty. Bewilderment spread over his beet-face as he ran his hands over Firpo's clothes. "What the hell did you do with it?"

"I didn't touch it," said Firpo.

"Take your duds off!"

Firpo Cole shed his clothes till he stood completely naked. Simms carefully felt and looked over each item of clothing and even ran his hands through Firpo's hair and looked in his mouth. The brooch was not on him. Simms gave the shivering Firpo permission to dress.

Then the department men carefully combed the room for any possible hiding place. The search did not reveal the missing jewel. Simms scratched at his chin, puzzled.

"Sure as hell that thing was on her neck when we come in here," he said.

Max asked: "Are you sure it was there when Firpo touched her?"

They looked at each other uncertainly, even suspiciously. Finally, Simms said: "Well, we know that Firpo hasn't got it." He jerked a finger at the reporters. "Search those crumbs down to their drawers. If it ain't on them you better take this room apart till you find it!"

Simms grabbed Firpo by the arm and pushed him toward the door. He never felt Firpo's sensitive, experienced fingers as they dipped into his jacket pocket to retrieve the missing brooch.

ALONE IN a small cell in the city jail, Firpo Cole hid the brooch in one of his shoes, then lay down on the iron cot and waited. He tried not to think of the dead body. It would just make him sick again and he couldn't afford that now. Afterwards it would be all right but first there was work to do.

Several hours passed and it was nearing ten before a guard came along and roused Firpo out of his dull, lethargic sleep. He blinked as he was taken into a sunlit, cheerful room. Simms sat behind a desk talking with Jugger Callahan and Ephraim Tuttle. There were a few cops there, including Max, and a male secretary was taking notes on a stenotype. The guard pushed Firpo into a chair and left.

Jugger was saying: "I didn't see her after she left with Firpo. Firpo used to walk her home every night so it was nothing out of the ordinary. Lots of crumbs hang out in front of every dance hall and she never liked to go home alone."

Simms asked: "Didn't you have another joint which burned down a couple of months ago?"

"Yes. I have a new place now. What of it?"

"Nothing. I just remembered. Was Ruth Bailey on the weed?"

"Not that I know of."

"The autopsy'll show anyway." Simms absently tore at a blotter. "It still looks like Firpo did it. He was nuts about Ruth Bailey but she passed him up for you."

Jugger's words came clipped and precise. "Ruth Bailey and I were friends and nothing more. Understand?"

Simms shrugged. "It makes no difference what you call it. Any way you slice it the motive is still jealousy. Last night Firpo got particularly jealous when he saw some guy talking to her through a few dances. Afterwards he picked a fight with the guy and got poked. He was mad clear through so he stole the letter opener and took her home and let her have it."

"That don't hold water," Ephraim Tuttle intruded. "My letter opener was missing *before* Firpo had that fight."

Simms carefully dropped the shreds of the blotter into a waste basket. "Before-after-sooner-later. What's the difference so long as he hangs for it?"

"I still think you're all wet about Firpo," said Jugger Callahan. "I'll be glad to stand the bail for him if he's held."

Simms pushed his chair back. "There ain't no bail in a first degree homicide charge."

Jugger Callahan and Ephraim Tuttle moved for the door. The band leader said to Firpo, "Take it easy," and they left.

Simms came from behind the desk and planted himself in front of Firpo. Max and one of the other cops moved in closer.

Simms spoke persuasively, almost with a note of regret: "It's open and shut, Firpo. If you get a good shyster you'll probably be able to beat it with an insanity plea. Sick guys like you who don't rate with the dames often get violent about it. You suddenly got tired of playing second fiddle to Jugger Callahan with the Bailey frill so you stole the letter opener. You had a chance to steal it any time because you were always around the Tango Palace. You walked her home, went up to her room and killed her."

Simms went over to a water cooler and drank three times from a lily cup.

Max said: "Firpo thought he wiped his prints off that letter opener but we'll bring 'em up with a special process."

Simms returned. "It had to be you, Firpo," he continued, "because anyone coming along later would have found Bailey in bed and she was wearing her street clothes when she was killed. What makes the whole thing worse is that you stole the letter opener beforehand so that makes it premeditated murder. Why don't you plead guilty, Firpo, and we'll let you cop an insanity plea?"

Firpo Cole didn't reply. The dick's words made him wonder why Ruth was still wearing her clothes when she was murdered. Ordinarily, she would have gone to bed right away. She was tired enough. Did she stay up to wait for Jugger? Did she go out to visit him and then come back?

Simms sighed. He said: "I hate to do this." He slapped Firpo squarely over the mouth and someone behind Firpo hit him over the ear. "Are you gonna look at this sensibly?" asked Simms.

The stenotypist left. The brooch was cutting into the sole of Firpo's foot but he was glad to feel it there. That cheap piece of jewelry which Jugger Callahan had bought for Mona Leeds would yet prove his guilt.

Simms hit Firpo over the mouth again and repeated his question. Blood from a broken tooth choked Firpo and he could only shake his head in reply. Somebody gave him a sharp, clipping blow over the nape of his neck, the chair tilted and the broadloom rug seemed to rush up at him.

"Like hitting an old woman," commented Max disgustedly.

WHEN FIRPO Cole regained consciousness, he found himself lying on the cot in his cell. The tooth socket had stopped bleeding. He did not know how long he stayed there. Somebody brought him a tin platter full of some mush but he didn't touch it. A drunk in the next cell tried to find out from Firpo what had caused the Yankees to slump.

After a while, the guard came along and he was taken up to that cheerful room again. Simms, Max and the other shams were there but this time the outsider was the stranger who had sat through eight dances with Ruth and who had subsequently biffed Firpo.

"Sit down, Firpo." Simms sounded friendly.

He indicated the stranger. "This is Mickey Hymer."

"I met him," responded Firpo through bruised lips.

"So you did. How come you tried to step on Mr. Hymer last night?"

"He wouldn't pay Ruth Bailey her tickets."

"As it turned out, Firpo, she didn't need them. Mr. Hymer is an investigator for Easternstates Insurance and he wants to ask you a few questions."

Mr. Hymer reached over and extended a hand to Firpo Cole. "First how about letting bygones be bygones?"

Firpo ignored the outstretched hand.

"Have it your way," shrugged the insurance dick. "Firpo, I'll be frank with you. We think that was no accidental fire that burned down the Tango Palace. Jugger Callahan had a pretty heavy policy on it and the whole business stinks."

Firpo Cole felt a sudden surge of panic. Jugger Callahan in jail for incendiarism and insurance fraud was the last thing he wanted. Jugger had to be kept free—and very accessible. He said: "That fire was on the level."

"What makes you think so, Firpo?"

"Jugger had over twelve hundred bucks in his desk when the place burned down. It was the take for three days and he was going to deposit it the next morning. If he would have started that fire he wouldn't have left that much dough there."

Mr. Hymer nodded. "That's the story I heard, Firpo, but Callahan had a heavy property policy on the place and that more than made up for the money that burned. Besides," he added with careful emphasis, "outside of Jugger Callahan's business manager, we have no proof that the money was really left there."

"What stinks about the fire?" asked Firpo.

"We found what looks like the remains of a few empty oil cans in the basement. In addition, it was a very profitable fire for Callahan. But what I'd like to know from you is where Ruth Bailey came in on it."

"Don't think you can frame her because she's dead," said Firpo tensely.

"Keep cool," soothed Mr. Hymer. "I got as much respect for the dead as the next man. Only I know she was the last one in the dance hall before it burned down and I thought maybe she told you something she forgot to say to me."

"She told me nothing you don't know. When she got home that night she found out that she forgot her purse at the dance hall so she had to go back."

"Why couldn't she get it the next day?"

"Because the key to her apartment was in it," said Firpo.

"I see. What's the rest of her story?"

"When she got back the place was empty and outside of a couple of lights someone left on, she saw nothing suspicious. She got her purse and went home. That's all she had to do with it."

Firpo wondered what the insurance dick would say if he knew that Ruth had taken that brooch from Jugger's office. Did it prove that Jugger Callahan had also come back after the others were gone and forgotten it on his desk?

Mr. Hymer picked at his nose thoughtfully. "That's the same story she—the deceased—told me last night." He stood up. "I guess I'll mosey along."

WHEN THE door was closed behind the insurance dick, Simms turned to Firpo. "It still looks like you're the murderer," he informed him cozily.

"I didn't do it," said Firpo Cole for the sake of the secretary's record.

"My men have been checking all morning and they can't find anyone who saw Ruth Bailey go out after you took her home last night. So you must have gone up to the apartment with her and killed her before she had a chance to get her clothes off and go to bed."

Suddenly, Firpo Cole knew the meaning of the lipstick on the dead woman's mouth. It was something no one could have noticed but he. He knew the kind of lipstick she

always used—a deep carmine brand named *Machiavelli*.
On those rare occasions that Ruth had kissed him, he had
never wiped it off. But the lipstick on her, when she was
murdered, had a tangerine coloring—the kind that Mona
Leeds, the torch singer, used. It could mean only that Ruth
had gone out again to see Mona.

Firpo hadn't been listening to Simms' persuasive arguments for appointing him the murderer. He said: "Go jump
in a sewer."

Simms and Max came around to where Firpo sat. The
stenotypist left the room. Firpo braced himself.

Simms sighed. "This is a hell of a case. I wish I knew what
happened to that jewelry that was on Bailey's neck." Then
he began to hit Firpo methodically, with semi-clenched
fists.

A spasm of coughing shook Firpo's spare body. The
coughs were heavy and deep from the lungs.

Max moved away. "Watch those damned germs," he
complained. "You oughta learn enough to cover your
mouth."

Firpo knew he was going to faint again. He struggled
against it, for a few moments, then gave way.

When Firpo Cole came around, he found himself
lying on a cot in the dispensary. He could see through an
unshaded window ahead of him. It was dark outside. He
must have been out for several hours.

The doctor who was bending over Firpo stood up and
faced Simms and Max. "He's all right now but if you give
him another shellacking I'm not responsible."

"Shellacking!" exclaimed Simms. "We hardly touched
the guy. We just gave him a few slaps to help his memory
and—"

"I'm not interested," cut in the doctor. "All I say is that another memory course might bring on a much worse hemorrhage, so don't try it." He snapped his bag shut and stalked over to a desk to fill in a report.

"And that's what you call cooperation," muttered Max.

Firpo sat up on the edge of the cot and buttoned his shirt. The telephone jangled and Max took it. He listened a moment, then tendered the receiver to Simms. "It's for you. The autopsy report on the Bailey woman."

"Yes?" said Simms. He glanced covertly toward Firpo. "You say that Ruth Bailey was opened by the usual mid-line incision? … You're some cut-up, ha, ha, ha … Now forget that scientific bull—tell me in plain, everyday American … I see … And how about her guts? … I see … Aha— the liver and spleen … and the markings on the body? … Good-looking, eh? … O.K., send up the report."

Simms cradled the receiver and turned to Firpo. "That sawbones just hasn't got any feelings."

"I know," said Firpo. "It's the psychological angle, so forget it."

"Wise guy. Well, what do you think about this? Ruth Bailey was gonna have a kid."

Firpo found some kind of medicine bottle within his reach and threw it.

Simms ducked. "A lie like that," he said darkly, "don't give you the right to throw things at me. Watch your step or I'll forget myself and give you the shellacking of your life. Now beat it."

"Beat it?" said Firpo stupidly.

"Yeah. Get out of here. We know damned well you did the murder but we can't prove it—yet. We're just giving you rope, Firpo."

Max emitted a sudden guffaw. "Maybe," he explained, "we'll give him more rope later—around the neck!"

CHAPTER THREE
REQUIEM IN JAZZ

LEAVING THE Hall of Justice, Firpo Cole cut across to old Chinatown. He dodged into a dark alley and pressed himself against the wall. He waited thus for fifteen minutes before he felt assured that he was not being followed. The cops didn't even have enough on him to put a shadow on his tail.

He removed his shoe and took out the brooch.

The sole of his foot was criss-crossed with cuts and his cotton sock was caked with blood. He bound the foot with a soiled handkerchief and proceeded up Main Street.

Some ten minutes later he reached a pawn shop just as the owner was closing up for the night. He put the brooch on the counter.

"I want you to look at this, Saul."

"Firpo, when will you guys learn I don't handle hot stuff?"

"I only asked you to look at it."

The short, bald-headed man picked up the brooch and studied it. Finally, he said: "I wouldn't touch it, Firpo, but it's worth two or three hundred dollars."

Firpo started. "For that little gold and a little piece of glass? Are you sure?"

"Not for the gold, Firpo. It's for what you think is a piece of glass." Saul held it back to let the light of a lamp fall on it. Small white rays seemed to radiate from a flaw in its sparkling sky-blue center.

"It's a fair example of a star sapphire," continued Saul, "and if it wasn't hot you'd even be able to get up to four and a half hundred for it."

Firpo took the brooch from Saul's hand and walked out. This gave Jugger Callahan an even stronger motive to murder Ruth Bailey. The brooch was worth real dough— all the more reason for Jugger to be thoroughly enraged over its theft.

Firpo saw a clock over a bus depot. It was already after ten. He wasn't at all hungry but he hadn't eaten since the previous evening and he knew that he should have something. He found some loose change in his pockets and entered a cafeteria. With swollen lips he sipped a glass of buttermilk through a straw, and then he headed straight for the Tango Palace.

The taxi dance hall was going full blast. On the platform, Mona Leeds was giving her all to the *Basin Street Blues* and extra hostesses were on the floor to take care of the large, Saturday night trade.

Firpo Cole sank into the settee and his eyes automatically searched among the dancers for Ruth Bailey. Then he remembered. Some of the girls walked over to tell him that Ruth had been a good kid and that if they could do anything....

To one side, Simms was grilling the hostesses by turns. He saw Firpo and came over to him.

"I hope there's no hard feelings, Firpo."

"Who found the body, Simms?"

"The apartment door was left open and some tenant who came in at three thirty saw her on the floor."

"O.K."

"You don't look so good, Firpo. You're as white as a baby's behind. Why don't you go home?"

"Why don't you leave me alone?"

"Now don't take it that way, Firpo. Just regard me as a plainclothes dick who has to do his job."

Firpo said: "I love you with an overwhelming passion."

Simms snorted. "If you didn't do the murder a guy would think you'd try to help me find who did. But everybody in this stinkhole thinks I'm their enemy." He stalked off.

Mona finished her number and left the stand. Ephraim Tuttle scurried back and forth settling arguments when he found them and creating them when he didn't. He stopped by Firpo Cole.

"I heard you were out, Firpo. I tried to tell those dopes that you couldn't have done a thing like that to her."

"Thanks."

The business manager regarded Firpo's battered face and clucked sympathetically. "That's a hell of a way to treat you. As if you would have touched a hair of her head."

"We won't talk about it, Tuttle."

"Sure. She'd want us to forget it."

"That's right. Shut up."

Ephraim Tuttle muttered something under his breath and left. Firpo buried his face in his hands and sobs seemed to rack his body, but when his hands dropped away, his eyes were dry. Rocco Pace, dressed to the hilt, came by and sat beside him.

The racketeer asked: "Are you still a checking-room?"

"Sure."

Rocco Pace slipped his gun out of the shoulder holster and handed it to Firpo. "I see that the shams gave you the lumps, pal."

Firpo Cole nodded.

"Don't let it worry you, Firpo. You'll get used to it—after a while." He patted Firpo's back and went out on the dance floor. In a moment, he was dancing a wild waltz, to the beat of a fox trot, whirling in and out among the unmoving couples.

FIRPO COLE ran fingers over the automatic in his pocket. He caressed its smoothness and put down the safety. He stood up and pushed his way through the dancers and idlers, down the length of the hall. He went through a curtained archway that led backstage to the band platform and knocked on the dressing-room off the right wings.

Mona Leeds said: "Come in."

He entered the small dressing-room. The torch singer was buffing her nails before the mirror.

"I'm glad they let you go, Firpo." The rich, husky voice sounded strained.

He took a cigarette from a case on a table and sat down. "They had to. They didn't have anything on me."

"You shouldn't smoke cigarettes, Firpo. They're not good for you."

He laughed.

"I know," she said rapidly. "You feel you don't give a damn any more. I'd feel that way if something happened to Jugger but it's wrong, Firpo. I don't know how to tell you but—" She floundered for the right words. "You can't know how sorry I am about the quarrel I had with Ruth last night. It was just a crazy fit of jealousy."

"Don't let it worry you, Mona. You couldn't help it and even Ruth wasn't mad about it."

"Firpo, if only we could find out who did it."

"Don't let that worry you either, Mona. What'd you tell the cops?"

"Just what happened," she replied. "I had that argument with Ruth and I never saw her again."

"That's a lie," said Firpo Cole deliberately. "I took Ruth home about one thirty. She probably went right out again and visited you. She didn't bring her purse along and before she left you she probably said that she looked like the wrath of God and—"

"Those were her exact words," uttered Mona Leeds softly.

He gave a wry grin. "Don't be surprised. I know Ruth. Anyway, you loaned her your powder and lipstick and she came home. That couldn't have been later than three in the morning. Somebody was either waiting for her at the apartment or followed her home and killed her. What I want to know is why you keep that visit to you a secret."

"You won't like it, Firpo. That's why I kept it to myself."

"I'm not a very sensitive plant. Go on."

"Well, she came to tell me she was sorry about our fight—and that she was a thief. She said she went back to the dance hall the night the old place burned down and found a piece of jewelry that Jugger had bought for me."

Firpo produced the brooch and showed it to the torch singer. "Is this what Ruth was talking about?"

"Yes—but she was wearing it on her dress. How did you get it?"

"That's a trade secret. Go on."

"Ruth took it from Jugger's desk," continued the torch singer, "and she came over last night to give it to me. I wouldn't take it."

"Why not?" he asked.

"Because it wasn't mine. Jugger might have bought it for me but he never mentioned it, so I told her to keep it—a sort of peace offering for that fight we had. I guess Jugger thinks it got lost in the fire."

Firpo Cole shook his head. "Jugger must have seen her wearing it."

"I guess so," replied Mona Leeds. "That's the way Jugger is. If he figured that she wanted it enough to steal it, he'd let her keep it."

"It's worth four or five hundred bucks, Mona, so I doubt it. You know, the Easternstates Insurance thinks the fire wasn't an accident."

The torch singer's hand went to her mouth in a frightened gesture. "No. Jugger wouldn't do a thing like that."

"How do you know?"

"But it's crazy, Firpo. He had a lot of money in his office—the receipts of a couple of days—that burned down, too."

"The insurance money more than made up for it. Besides, they're not so sure the money was there in the first place. They only have Jugger's and Tuttle's word for it."

"But why should he take such a chance for a few dollars, Firpo? He's doing fine the way he is."

"I don't know but I'll damned well find out." He stood up. "You're O.K., Mona. Don't take it too hard if I find out that Jugger killed Ruth."

He left her staring after him with wide-eyed apprehension.

FIRPO COLE entered on the right wings of the band platform, found a meeting chair and sat down. From where he was, he could watch Jugger Callahan fronting the band.

Jugger caught sight of Firpo, snapped his fingers to the boys and the music trailed off. He spoke into the mike.

"Ladies and gentlemen, last night one of our beloved hostesses met a tragic end and out of respect to her I'd like everybody to keep thirty seconds of real silence."

He bowed his head and checked his wrist-watch. Throughout the semi-dark hall, couples waited with their arms twined around each other. Some girl in the back giggled and said: "No."

The thirty seconds were up. Jugger Callahan's toes beat a tattoo and he snapped his fingers. "All right, boys. A one-a, a two-a, a three-a, scratch!" The band began *Potato Head Blues* and the couples started to sway again like puppets whose wires had suddenly been jerked.

Jugger walked over to Firpo. He patted his greased-back hair, obviously pleased that he had done the right thing by Ruth.

"Firpo," said the band leader, "we already got sixty-two bucks collected. How much can you chip in?"

"For what?"

"Ruth's funeral, of course," replied Jugger.

"I'm not interested in Ruth's funeral. There's somebody else's funeral I want to see about."

"Uh-huh. I get you, Firpo, but you ought to leave that to the cops. You probably never even met the guy who did it."

Firpo's bloodshot eyes fixed themselves on the band leader's face. "I won't have far to go. That letter opener was stolen from here."

"Say, that's right, isn't it? Ephraim come to me around eleven thirty last night and asked me if I'd taken it so it must have been stolen earlier."

Firpo's hands were in his pockets. There was something friendly and comforting about the feel of the automatic. He said: "We'll talk about it later."

"Sure, Firpo," said Jugger, not too heartily. "Sure."

The band leader returned to his post. The music ground on. Twenty sets, of three melodies each, every hour. Sixty dances in as many minutes with only an occasional break to give the customers a chance to buy more tickets.

The *Smiling Troubadours* never stopped playing, though every once in a while a musician left the stand. And, as the hours wore on and they became more tired, the music became faster and more frenzied.

Firpo stayed in his chair, watching the band leader. He didn't intend letting Jugger out of his sight—not till he could trap him some way and prove to himself that here was the murderer of Ruth Bailey.

Simms reached backstage in the course of his investigations. He seemed as much in a fog as ever. He asked Firpo whether Ruth had had any jewelry on her dress when he'd seen the body. Firpo couldn't remember and the police dick left.

The time went by and Firpo sat unmoving, watching Jugger Callahan with lackluster eyes. He tried to think of the murder of the only person he had ever cared for. What had Ruth said? That she was afraid? Of what?

Suddenly, it hit Firpo Cole like a ton of dynamite. Where was the five hundred dollars that had found its way into Ruth Bailey's purse and where was the envelope that read: *This better be enough?*

The police hadn't said anything about the money or envelope so the murderer must have stolen both. There was no reason why the killer shouldn't have taken the money but the envelope was a different matter. That typewritten sentence on it meant something to the murderer. Someone in the Tango Palace had probably thought that Ruth Bailey was blackmailing him. That very envelope had probably been written on one of the office typewriters.

Firpo frowned and the swollen lips pursed in thought. His job was to find out who had typed that envelope.

AT TWO in the morning, the *Smiling Troubadours* gradually, almost reluctantly, stopped playing. There seemed to be a kind of weary excitement among them after the long grind. Customers filed out, spotlights went off and hostesses sat down to nurse their feet.

Firpo Cole fell into step beside Jugger Callahan as the band leader talked to friends, visited the washroom and finally went to his office. Jugger did not object. He imagined that Firpo felt lost—that he needed friendship. Firpo was like a dog that had lost its master and was trying to attach itself to someone else.

After Jugger had finished checking the night's receipts with the business manager, he turned to Firpo. "We're having a tea party tonight. How about coming along? A couple of reefers might do you good."

Tea parties were a custom of long standing on every Saturday night at Jugger Callahan's apartment. Any other time, Firpo Cole would have felt highly honored by the invitation, for these parties were attended only by the elite of the Tango Palace.

"I wouldn't miss it for the world," said Firpo.

Ephraim Tuttle locked up the books, said he'd see them later and went to pay off the girls. Firpo and the band leader left the dance hall. They walked down Main, then turned up Sixth.

"Jugger," asked Firpo Cole, "can you typewrite?"

"One finger stuff. Why?"

"It's not important. Is there a file up in the office listing the girls' addresses?"

"Of course."

"Then anyone at the Tango could find out where Ruth lived."

"I guess so, Firpo, but—"

"You could find out, too, couldn't you?" cut in Firpo.

"What the hell are you getting at?"

"Forget it, Jugger."

The band leader started to say something but stayed his reply. They turned in to an all-night drugstore. Here, for a fiver, the clerk forgot the narcotic laws and gave Jugger a twelve-ounce bottle of *cannabis indica*. The band leader then bought a carton of cigarettes and some brown cigarette paper.

They went outside and hailed a taxi.

CHAPTER FOUR
PAID IN FULL

JUGGER CALLAHAN'S apartment was large and comfortable. Most of the boys from the band were already there. Mona Leeds and Evelyn Dorn, Ephraim Tuttle's current doll, were making and serving sandwiches to the guests. Jugger lolled in an overstuffed chair and Firpo sat right beside him watching the preparations.

Monkey Harris and a few of the other boys had sliced open the cigarettes from the carton and emptied the tobacco into a wide, shallow pan. Now they took the bottle of *cannabis indica* and poured the greenish-brown liquid into the pan. They allowed the tobacco to soak in the poisonous drug for several minutes, then put a match to it—which served both to burn up the excess alcohol and to dry the tobacco. This done, they began to wrap the residue in the brown cigarette paper. They worked diligently and the heap of these homemade marihuana cigarettes grew steadily.

Jugger said to Firpo Cole: "These give a much better kick than the ready made kind."

"I never tried them," replied Firpo. "When did you first start?" He wanted to hear Jugger talk—to wait for that mistake, that slip of the tongue which would point the finger of guilt at him.

Jugger Callahan was in an expansive mood. He said: "Back in Chi, in the Capone days. A bunch of us muggle-hounds would get together and play hot music long before the word 'swing' was ever invented. Today the high school punks have taken over. They call themselves jitterbugs and if we sound good we're out of this world. They call the clarinet a licorice stick, a trombone a grunt iron, the bass fiddle a doghouse—and most of the time I don't know what the hell they're talking about."

"Yeah," said Firpo. "Those sure were the good old days, all right, in Chi."

"The only thing that flowed freer than money," continued the band leader reminiscently, "was blood. We used to have classy apartments and buy a lot of jewelry for our women."

Firpo suddenly reached into his pocket and held the brooch out. "You mean like this thing you bought for Mona?"

Jugger Callahan didn't bite. "I bought that for Mona? What you getting at, Firpo?"

"Haven't you ever seen it before?" asked Firpo Cole.

"No—yes, I think Ruth Bailey wore something like that."

Firpo frowned. Jugger was too old a hand to be caught that crudely. He said: "This is a star sapphire. It's pretty valuable."

Evelyn Dorn was hovering over them with a sandwich tray. Her doe eyes bulged. "Geeze! A star sapphire." She took it and examined it reverently. "That's what I always wanted to get—a star sapphire." She sighed. "But I guess I ain't got what it takes. Nobody's given me any—not even one yet."

"I'd still like to know what you were getting at, Firpo," said the band leader.

Firpo retrieved the brooch. "Let's drop it."

Evelyn Dorn suddenly snapped her fingers. "Hell, Firpo, I forgot to tell you!"

"What?"

"That gangster—that Rocco Pace is on the warpath after you. You better watch out."

"What's the matter now?" asked Jugger.

"That's all right," said Firpo. "It's nothing to worry about. I just stole Rocco's gun."

Jugger Callahan looked at him queerly but made no comment. Evelyn Dorn wandered off. Firpo leaned back and closed his eyes. An idea was stirring within him.

Turnip Billings, who played tenor horn, called out: "All finished, boys. Jugger Callahan and his Twelve Shtoonks will now get high."

He tossed a few reefers to Firpo Cole and Jugger Callahan.

JUGGER CALLAHAN was a breather and it was not long before a quiet contentment seemed to come over him. After a while, he fixed glazed eyes on Firpo and said: "You're not running after me because you like my mustache. You think I killed Ruth Bailey."

Firpo Cole, who was bluffing his smoke, nodded.

"What'll you do about it?"

"When I make sure, I'll kill you." Firpo's voice was dispassionate but as certain of itself as a pile driver.

Jugger Callahan laughed. His good humor was not even ruffled. "You two-bit grifter, you talk big. How come you think I killed your Ruth Bailey?"

"She was in love with you, Jugger—really in love—the way a bum like you couldn't understand."

"I liked Ruth, but that's all, Firpo. I never two-timed on Mona."

"I know," replied Firpo. "I would of made you marry Ruth if you had."

The band leader laughed again. "Pickpocket to marriage broker. That's good. But you haven't told me how you think I come to kill Ruth."

They were talking in low tones. The others around them still laughed and shouted boisterously. The drug had not yet begun to take effect.

Firpo said: "I figure it this way. You put a lot of insurance on the old Tango Palace and then faked a fire by soaking the drapes and everything else in oil and gasoline."

"You better keep those ideas to yourself," said Jugger Callahan a little more seriously.

"I don't have to. An insurance dick thinks that. He found what used to be oil cans in the ruins. You also forgot that stone I showed you on your desk, because Ruth had to go back to the Palace that night and she saw it there. You must have been fixing for the fire about that time and you probably saw her take it."

"So now you're calling Ruth Bailey a crook."

Firpo's hands began to tremble and he waited a few moments before replying. "She took it because she knew you bought it for Mona and she was jealous. She started wearing it every day after that, Jugger, just to get Mona's goat but you thought it was her way of saying that she knew you started that fire."

"Not so fast, Firpo. I lost over twelve hundred dollars in cold cash during the fire and you don't think I'd be crazy enough to leave it up there if I burned the place down."

"I know that angle too, Jugger, but there's no proof you left the dough to burn and that it isn't in your pocket right now."

"Well, I'll be damned," the band leader uttered softly. "And what do you think I did after the fire?"

"Ruth was wearing that thing and you thought she was blackmailing you so you tried to buy her off. You slipped five hundred bucks into her purse with a note saying that it better be enough. But she kept wearing the brooch and you thought she wanted more sugar so you stole Tuttle's letter opener, figuring that anyone at the Palace could be blamed. Then you killed her with it. It had a sharp point. It must have been easy."

"That's a lot of shtush, Firpo, and you know it. You're just excited about the killing. When you have a good night's sleep you'll decide you couldn't prove a thing."

"That's the only reason you're still alive, Jugger."

Ephraim Tuttle had come in and walked over to them in time to hear the last sentence. "What's going on?" he asked.

"Firpo's puking about some kind of star sapphire and that I killed Ruth Bailey," responded Jugger.

"Oh, he's just weed-wacky," pronounced the business manager. "I don't know why the hell we let him louse up the place around here." He walked away.

THE DOORBELL to the apartment rang. Mona Leeds came in from the kitchen and said: "See who it is, Firpo." He went through the vestibule. It was Rocco Pace standing at the door.

"I thought I'd find you here," said the racketeer.

"Do you want to come in?"

"That ain't what I'm here for. I get a plenty good jag with dago-red."

"Then what did you want?" asked Firpo.

"Why'd you hook my gat?"

"I want to borrow it for a while, Rocco." Rocco Pace gave a vague smile.

"You liked that jane a lot, didn't you, Firpo?"

"Yes."

"I see. And you have to go gunning with my rod."

"I'll give it back to you after, Rocco."

"Let's have it now."

"I said I want to keep it for a while."

Rocco Pace's voice was silken. "You know better than to give me any backtalk, Firpo. Let's have it."

Firpo Cole hesitated a moment, then surrendered. "O.K.," he said bleakly and handed the automatic to the racketeer.

Rocco Pace whipped a polka-dotted handkerchief out of his breast pocket and carefully wiped the gun. Then he returned it to Firpo. "You ought to know better than to sport a rod with my prints on it." He started off, then paused. "I don't know if it'll help you, Firpo, but one of the guys up at the Tango Palace has been plunging pretty heavily with a bookie I know. It's practically bankrupted him. You can have it for what it's worth."

"Who is it?"

"I blowed my whistle plenty. It ought to satisfy you."

"Thanks, Rocco. You're white."

"Think nothing of it," said the racketeer breezily.

Firpo Cole returned to the living-room.

The tea party was in full session. All the lights were out but for a small, red bulb in a floor lamp. Firpo could distinguish the figures as they moved only to lift the reefers to their mouth for short, quick puffs. Mona Leeds reclined next to Jugger, in the easy chair that Firpo had vacated.

An expensive phonograph was playing repeats of a swing record as slowly as it was able. The record was Armstrong's version of *Knockin a Jug* and in one corner Monkey Harris was beating an accompaniment on a tom-tom. His slim, yellowed fingers beat rapidly. The test of a good musician, on these occasions, was the number of beats and variations the player could get in, between two chords—and Monkey Harris was rated highly.

The effect was weird as the disk revolved and the tom-tom beat. The record was played slowly and the reefers themselves tended to slow and dull everything—thereby providing for a full appreciation of the music. And every so often a musician grunted or delivered an "Oh" or an "Ah" as he caught some new nuance in the music that he'd never before heard.

The air was heavy with those pungent, cloying fumes and Firpo Cole began to cough. He didn't have to look at his handkerchief to know it was becoming smeared with red.

But he didn't care. At last he knew what was what. That small item of information from Rocco Pace had done the trick. The coughing became worse and he walked into the kitchen.

EVELYN DORN was wolfing minced ham sandwiches. "I'd rather eat here than get sick in there," she explained.

Firpo Cole said: "Inside you were raving about star sapphires. Did you ever ask Tuttle to give you one?"

"Sure. It don't harm to ask—but I never got it."

"That's what I thought. Tuttle did buy it for you, Evelyn, only he forgot it at the old place when it burned down."

"No kiddin'?"

"He's bought you a lot of stuff, hasn't he?"

"Some," she said coyly. "Ephraim ain't a tightwad."

"That's what I figured—and on top of that he's been playing the horses. That's why he set that fire and later killed Ruth."

Evelyn Dorn stopped eating for a moment. "You mean it?"

Firpo nodded. "He stole twelve hundred bucks in receipts from Jugger and then burned the joint down. He figured rightly that Jugger would think the money burned with the building and that he was making enough profit on insurance not to investigate too much."

"Well, what do you know?" marveled Evelyn.

Firpo's voice became bitter. "When Tuttle stole that dough from Jugger's office he accidentally left that brooch which he bought for you on Jugger's desk—and that's where Ruth found it. He made a too-big stink about losing his letter opener and then killed Ruth with it. He thought she was blackmailing him about the fire and wasn't satisfied with a five-hundred-buck payoff."

"You can never tell about someone," she commented. "Can you?"

The double-hinge door swung open and Simms, the police detective, Max and Ephraim Tuttle came in.

"All right, Firpo," said Simms. "I know you got that jewelry you stole from Bailey's body. Let's have it."

The automatic appeared in Firpo's hand. The safety catch was still off—the way he wanted it. "Stick your mitts up and line against the wall."

The three men did as they were bid. Evelyn Dorn gave a squeal and fled. They could hear the apartment door slam shut.

"Now look here, Firpo," Simms' voice was hoarse. "This ain't gonna help. If you just take it easy—"

"Can it," interrupted Firpo. "I suppose Tuttle told you I had the brooch."

Simms nodded.

Tuttle said quickly: "I didn't mean anything, Firpo. I just heard it was stolen and then when Jugger said you was talking about it I thought I better call the cops."

Firpo's voice was as calm and as steady as the hand that held the gun. "Tuttle, all you figured was that you'd pin the killing on me and get out of it yourself. But there's no chance of that because you're paying for it now." He took a bead on the pit of Ephraim Tuttle's stomach.

"Now watch it," said Simms rapidly. "Let us take care of it, Firpo. If he did the killing he's entitled to a trial but sure as hell you'll swing if you try it yourself."

"I know I will," said Firpo Cole, "and this'll be one condemned man that'll really eat a damned hearty breakfast."

Then he sighted carefully and pulled the trigger six times.

ABOUT THE AUTHOR

I AM twenty-seven years old and much as I would like to hint at prospecting the Gold Coast or gun-running below the Rio Grande, I cannot. Simply, then: I have done nothing of especial interest.

I was born in Manhattan and raised on the South shore of Long Island where I attended the elementary and secondary schools.

I worked at carpentry and cabinet- and candy-making and drove an armored Post Office truck and carried (as per regulations) a Colt .45 that scared the living daylights out of me.

Then came "higher" education, at New York University. There, amidst the sylvan glades (Washington Square Branch) I studied Anthropology, History and English without neglecting the serial "cliff-hangers" at a nearby Eight Avenue grind house. Eventually I secured an A.B.

Armed thus with a degree and the intellectual assets of eye-glasses and a receding hair-line, I managed to become an outside reader for Fox Films and thereafter drifted into reading for Broadway play brokers.

For the next few years (when not visiting with my family in Hollywood) I haunted New York's theatrical byways, working as a casting director, at play doctoring, an assistant producer, and a stage manager. At one time I was stage manager for the Theatre Guild and at a lot of other times I wasn't.

During those years I stocked my shelves with rejected stories and articles.

www.ingramcontent.com/pod-product-compliance
Lightning Source LLC
Chambersburg PA
CBHW030539030726
47495CB00004B/1058